THE STORM

"What just happened?" Carter shouted.

"Did we hit some rocks?" Buzz asked.

"Dad!" Vanessa shouted. "Dad? Can you hear me?" She started scrambling through the pile of debris on the floor, but she couldn't find the phone anywhere.

Instead, her hand landed in cold water. It was soaking the carpet, Vanessa realized. When she looked to her right, she saw it was also pouring in from under the small engine-compartment door.

At the same moment, Joe came barreling down the galley steps.

"What are you doing?" Vanessa asked. "Joe, where's Dex? There's water coming in!"

But Joe wasn't listening. He was holding the side-band radio transmitter with one hand and adjusting a dial on the console with the other.

"SOS, SOS, this is the *Lucky Star*," Joe said into the handset. "SOS, SOS, this is the *Lucky Star*, do you copy?"

Whatever was said next, Vanessa didn't hear. It was swallowed up by a brilliant flash of lightning and a crash of thunder too overwhelming to be anywhere but right on top of them.

In the next moment, the entire cabin was thrown into darkness.

The STRANDED Series

Book 1: STRANDED
Book 2: TRIAL BY FIRE
Book 3: SURVIVORS

STRANDED
SHADOW ISLAND

Book 1: FORBIDDEN PASSAGE
Book 2: THE SABOTAGE
Book 3: DESPERATE MEASURES

JEFF PROBST

and CHRIS TEBBETTS

PUFFIN BOOKS
An Imprint of Penguin Group (USA)

PUFFIN BOOKS
Published by the Penguin Group
Penguin Group (USA) LLC
375 Hudson Street
New York, New York 10014

USA * Canada * UK * Ireland * Australia
New Zealand * India * South Africa * China

penguin.com
A Penguin Random House Company

First published in the United States of America by Puffin Books,
an imprint of Penguin Young Readers Group, 2013

LIBRARY OF CONGRESS CATALOGING-IN-PUBLICATION DATA IS AVAILABLE.

Puffin Books ISBN 978-0-14-242424-7

Design by Tony Sahara

Printed in the United States of America

13 15 17 19 20 18 16 14 12

Dedicated to Michael & Ava

It was my wife, Lisa, who had the original idea for this series. It came from a desire to share stories of blended families living out amazing adventures. Whatever type of family you have, we hope it inspires you!

—JP

STRANDED

CHAPTER 1

It was day four at sea, and as far as eleven-year-old Carter Benson was concerned, life didn't get any better than this.

From where he hung, suspended fifty feet over the deck of the *Lucky Star*, all he could see was a planet's worth of blue water. The boat's huge white mainsail ballooned in front of him, filled with a stiff southerly wind that sent them scudding through the South Pacific faster than they'd sailed all week.

This was the best part of the best thing Carter had ever done, no question. It was like sailing and flying at the same time. The harness around his middle held him in place while his arms and legs hung free. The air itself seemed to carry him along, at speed with the boat.

"How you doin' up there, Carter?" Uncle Dexter shouted from the cockpit.

Carter flashed a thumbs-up and pumped his fist. "Faster!" he shouted back. Even with the wind whipping in his ears, Dex's huge belly laugh came back, loud and clear.

Meanwhile, Carter had a job to do. He wound the safety line from his harness in a figure eight around the cleat on the mast to secure himself. Then he reached over and unscrewed the navigation lamp he'd come up here to replace.

As soon as he'd pocketed the old lamp in his rain slicker, he pulled out the new one and fitted it into the fixture, making sure not to let go before he'd tightened it down. Carter had changed plenty of lightbulbs before, but never like this. If anything, it was all too easy and over too fast.

When he was done, he unwound his safety line and gave a hand signal to Dex's first mate, Joe

Kahali, down below. Joe put both hands on the winch at the base of the mast and started cranking Carter back down to the deck.

"Good job, Carter," Joe said, slapping him on the back as he got there. Carter swelled with pride and adrenaline. Normally, replacing the bulb would have been Joe's job, but Dex trusted him to take care of it.

Now Joe jerked a thumb over his shoulder. "Your uncle wants to talk to you," he said.

Carter stepped out of the harness and stowed it in its locker, just like Dex and Joe had trained him to do. Once that was done, he clipped the D-ring on his life jacket to the safety cable that ran the length of the deck and headed toward the back.

It wasn't easy to keep his footing as the *Lucky Star* pitched and rolled over the waves, but even that was part of the fun. If he did fall, the safety cable—also called a jackline—would keep him from going overboard. Everyone was required to stay clipped in when they were on deck, whether they were up there to work . . . or to puke, like Buzz was doing right now.

"Gross! Watch out, Buzz!" Carter said, pushing past him.

"*Uhhhhhnnnnh*," was all Buzz said in return. He was leaning against the rail and looked both green and gray at the same time.

Carter kind of felt sorry for him. They were both eleven years old, but they didn't really have anything else in common. It was like they were having two different vacations out here.

"Gotta keep moving," he said, and continued on toward the back, where Dex was waiting.

"Hey, buddy, it's getting a little choppier than I'd like," Dex said as Carter stepped down into the cockpit. "I need you guys to get below."

"I don't want to go below," Carter said. "Dex, I can help. Let me steer!"

"No way," Dex said. "Not in this wind. You've been great, Carter, but I promised your mom before we set sail—no kids on deck if these swells got over six feet. You see that?" He pointed to the front of the boat, where a cloud of sea spray had just broken over the bow. "*That's* what a six-foot swell looks like. We've got a storm on the way—maybe a big one. It's time for you to take a break."

"Come on, please?" Carter said. "I thought we came out here to sail!"

Dex took him by the shoulders and looked him square in the eye.

"Remember what we talked about before we set out? My boat. My rules. Got it?"

Carter got it, all right. Arguing with Dex was like wrestling a bear. You could try, but you were never going to win.

"Now, grab your brother and get down there," Dex told him.

"Okay, fine," Carter said. "But he's not my brother, by the way. Just because my mom married his dad doesn't mean—"

"Ask me tomorrow if I care," Dexter said, and gave him a friendly but insistent shove. "Now go!"

Benjamin "Buzz" Diaz lifted his head from the rail

and looked out into the distance. All he could see from here was an endless stretch of gray clouds over an endless stretch of choppy waves.

Keeping an eye on the horizon was supposed to help with the seasickness, but so far, all it had done was remind him that he was in the middle of the biggest stretch of nowhere he'd ever seen. His stomach felt like it had been turned upside down and inside out. His legs were like rubber bands, and his head swam with a thick, fuzzy feeling, while the boat rocked and rocked and rocked.

It didn't look like this weather was going to be changing anytime soon, either. At least, not for the better.

Buzz tried to think about something else—anything else—to take his mind off how miserable he felt. He thought about his room back home. He thought about how much he couldn't wait to get there, where he could just close his door and hang out all day if he wanted, playing City of Doom and eating pepperoni pizz—

Wait, Buzz thought. *No. Not that.*

He tried to unthink anything to do with food, but it was too late. Already, he was leaning over the rail again and hurling the last of his breakfast into the ocean.

"Still feeding the fish, huh?" Suddenly, Carter was back. He put a hand on Buzz's arm. "Come on," he said. "Dex told me we have to get below."

Buzz clutched his belly. "Are you kidding?" he said. "Can't it wait?"

"No. Comc on."

All week long, Carter had been running around the deck of the *Lucky Star* like he owned it or something. Still, Carter was the least of Buzz's worries right now.

It was only day four at sea, and if things kept going like this, he was going to be lucky to makc it to day five.

Vanessa Diaz sat at the *Lucky Star*'s navigation station belowdecks and stared at the laptop screen in front of her. She'd only just started to learn about this stuff a few days earlier, but as far as she could tell, all that orange and red on the weather radar was a bad sign. Not to mention the scroll across the bottom of the screen, saying something about "gale-force winds and deteriorating conditions."

The first three days of their trip had been nothing but clear blue skies and warm breezes. Now, nine hundred miles off the coast of Hawaii, all of that had changed. Dexter kept saying they had to adjust their course to outrun the weather, but so far, it seemed like the weather was outrunning them. They'd changed direction at least three times, and things only seemed to be getting worse.

The question was—how *much* worse?

A chill ran down Vanessa's spine as the hatch over the galley stairs opened, and Buzz and Carter came clattering down the steps.

"How are you feeling, Buzzy?" she asked, but he didn't stop to talk. Instead, he went straight for the little bathroom—the "head," Dexter called it—and slammed the door behind him.

Her little brother was getting the worst of these bad seas, by far. Carter, on the other hand, seemed unfazed.

Sometimes Vanessa called them "the twins," as a joke, because they were both eleven but nothing alike. Carter kept his sandy hair cut short and was even kind of muscley for a kid his age. Buzz, on the other hand, had shaggy jet-black curls like their father's and was what adults liked to call husky. The kids at school just called him fat.

Vanessa didn't think her brother was fat—not exactly—but you could definitely tell he spent a lot of time in front of the TV.

"It's starting to rain," Carter said, looking up at the sky.

"Then close the hatch," Vanessa said.

"Don't tell me what to do."

Vanessa rolled her eyes. "Okay, fine. Get wet. See if I care."

He would, too, she thought. He'd just stand there and get rained on, only because she told him not to. Carter was one part bulldog and one part mule.

Jane was there now, too. She'd just come out of the tiny sleeping cabin the two girls shared.

Jane was like the opposite of Carter. She could slip in and out of a room without anyone ever noticing. With Carter, you always knew he was there.

"What are you looking at, Nessa?" Jane asked.

"Nothing." Vanessa flipped the laptop closed. "I was just checking the weather," she said.

There was no reason to scare Jane about all that. She was only nine, and tiny for her age. Vanessa was the oldest, at thirteen, and even though nobody told her to look out for Jane on this trip, she did anyway.

"Dex said there's a storm coming," Carter blurted out. "He said it's going to be major."

"Carter!" Vanessa looked over at him and rolled her eyes in Jane's direction.

But he just shrugged. "What?" he said. "You think she's not going to find out?"

"You don't have to worry about me," Jane said.

She crawled up onto Vanessa's lap and opened the computer to have a look. "Show me."

"See?" Carter said. "I know my sister."

Vanessa took a deep breath. If the idea of this trip was to make them one big happy family, it wasn't exactly working.

Technically, the whole sailing adventure was a wedding gift from her new uncle, Dexter. It had been two months since Vanessa and Buzz's father had married Carter and Jane's mother, but they'd waited until the end of the school year to take a honeymoon. Now, while their parents were hiking Volcanoes National Park and enjoying the beaches on Hawaii's Big Island, the four kids were spending the week at sea and supposedly getting to know one another better.

So far, the sailing had been amazing, but the sister-brother bonding thing? Not so much, Vanessa thought. The weather wasn't helping, either. It looked like they were going to be cooped up together for the rest of the day.

"Is that the storm?" Jane said. She pointed at the large red mass on the laptop screen.

"That's it," Vanessa answered. On the computer, it seemed as if the oncoming front had gotten even bigger in the last few minutes. She started braiding Jane's long blond hair to distract her.

"It's just rain, right?" Jane said. "If this was something really bad, we'd already know about it. Wouldn't we, Nessa?"

Vanessa tried to smile. "Sure," she said. But the truth was, she had no idea how bad it was going to get.

None of them did.

CHAPTER 2

Jane sat on her bunk, with her back pressed against the wall to steady herself. The boat was rocking too hard to prop her camera on a shelf like she usually did. Instead, she held it out at arm's length and pressed Record.

"Hi, everyone. It's Jane B. again, reporting for Evanston Elementary."

It took more concentration to hold the camera steady than it did to say the words. "Today is June twenty-eighth, and it's the fourth day of our sailing trip. I don't know if you can tell, but the weather's not nearly as nice today. Here, I'll show you."

She held the camera up to the cabin's porthole to show the tossing waves outside. On the view screen, it looked as if the whole world were tilting back and forth.

She didn't need her whole class to know how scared she actually was. Not Vanessa and the boys, either. They all treated her like a baby to begin with. So she talked about other things instead.

"I read in one of Uncle Dexter's books that the Pacific Ocean is ten thousand miles across and has some of the strongest wind currents in the world," Jane narrated. "Less than one percent of the whole ocean is covered in land, so I guess there isn't much to stop the wind from blowing out here."

She'd done plenty of research for her report. She always did. Carter called her a brainiac for doing extra-credit work over summer vacation, but then again, Carter's best subject was gym.

Besides, it was something to do while this storm set in around them.

"Uncle Dexter says the weather can change really fast around here," Jane went on, as casually as she could. "In the meantime, there's not that much to tell. We're all just staying put and holding on tight. Dex calls it hunkering down, so I guess that's what we're going to do. Until later, this is Jane Benson, reporting from somewhere in the South Pacific."

By the time it started to get dark, Buzz was starting to feel normal again. Maybe the seasickness was finally behind him. Or maybe there just wasn't anything left to throw up, Buzz thought.

In any case, he still wasn't hungry. Nobody was. The weather had only gotten worse, and it seemed to have taken away everyone's appetite. The kids all spent the evening sitting around the galley table, holding on to the edges of things for balance as the boat rolled over the waves. Each time another one hit, it was like a jolt to the body.

While they waited for the storm to pass, Jane watched and rewatched all of the videos she'd made for her report so far. Vanessa sat and played the same game on her phone, over and over. She'd given up trying to text her friends days ago, when it became clear that there was no cell reception out here on the open ocean. Carter listened to music with his headphones on and practiced nautical knots with an old piece of rope.

Buzz just sat, listening to the wind whistling through the masts and the rain pelting the boat from all sides. He'd already run down the batteries on the handheld game he'd brought, along with his spare batteries. On top of that, without any sun all day, the boat's solar panel hadn't been able to generate any electricity at all for the *Lucky Star*. The only other source of power was the boat's engine, but Dexter wasn't keen to use that in the storm. Dexter had told everyone to conserve electricity until further notice. That meant no laptop, no DVDs, and as few lights as possible belowdecks.

Just after eight o'clock, when the cabin windows had gone completely dark, the hatch opened and Dexter came down the stairs. All week long, he'd been upbeat and smiley, like some kind of friendly giant who laughed at just about anything. But not now. His expression was grim as he ran a hand over his dripping-wet face.

"I hate to say it, guys, but it looks like this is going to get worse before it gets better. There's a crazy cold front playing heck with the forecasts. It's pushing some of this storm at us faster than we expected."

He stopped and held tight to the upright pole in the middle of the salon as the boat dipped and rose, and dipped again. Coffee mugs clattered against one another in the cabinet. Jane's camera slid across the table.

"This kind of thing's always a possibility, but not to worry," Dexter went on. "The only thing to do now is sit tight while we skirt around this squall a little farther."

"Does that mean we're changing course again?" Vanessa asked.

"Yep," Dex said. He went to the nav station, unrolled a chart, and looked at it. "But just temporarily. Today's Boomerang Day, and I'll have us right back on track by tomorrow."

Boomerang Day was Dex's name for the trip's midpoint, when they came around and headed back toward Hawaii. Maybe that was a good thing, Buzz thought. It meant they'd gotten half of this trip over with. Then again, it also meant that they were as far from home as they'd ever been.

When Dex looked up from his chart, he seemed to sense something in their faces. He turned toward the group again with his hands clasped in front of him.

"Guys, I think your parents would be proud to see how brave you're all being. I know it's scary, but you've got me and Joe up top, handling everything. I just need you to be down here, for one another. Make sense?"

"Yeah," Vanessa said quietly. Carter shrugged.

"Carter?" Dex said, leaning down to catch his eyes. "You got a problem with that?"

"No," Carter said. "I just wish I could help."

"You can help," he said. "Down here. Right now,

your job is to hang tough, and hang together, so you're ready to go when we need you on deck again."

Buzz looked down at the table, trying not to show his face. He didn't feel very tough right now.

"You know what?" Dex said. "I'm almost glad this storm came up."

That seemed to get everyone's attention.

"Why?" Jane asked.

"I've sailed with some rough-and-tumble crews before—even rougher than you four," he said with a wink. "I remember this one time, we were out fishing, a couple hundred miles north of Oahu. We got hit with the biggest, fastest-moving squall I've ever seen. It was like sailing sideways, with enough wind to blow you right off the deck. That storm made this one look like a little spring shower, and I don't think any of us thought we were going to see the morning."

"Um . . . Dex?" Buzz said. "I thought you said you were glad this storm came up."

"Right," he said. "My point is, we all pulled together that night and made it through. Not only that, but those guys are still some of my best buddies. A hard turn like this just brings you closer together. And let's face it, isn't that exactly what your parents wanted you kids to get out of this trip?"

Just then, the small companionway door at the back of the rear sleeping cabin opened up, and Joe shouted down from the cockpit.

"Dex? Can you get up here? *Now?*"

"What is it?" Vanessa asked, the worry plain in her voice. "What's going on?"

"Probably just a loose line. I'll go find out," Dex said.

"You sure you don't want some help?" Carter said. "I can hold the wheel."

Dexter turned and put out one of his big hands to stop Carter.

"There's nothing that needs doing right now," he said. "But I do want you guys to strap on your PFDs."

"What?" Buzz blurted out. PFD stood for

"personal flotation device"—also known as a life jacket. Dex already had his on, but he'd been working up top. "Why do we need those?"

"It's just standard operating procedure for a storm like this," Dexter said. "You never take chances on a boat." He pulled the four vests off the hooks where they hung by the stairs and dropped them on the galley table. Then he stopped, just long enough to show his old familiar smile. "There's nothing to worry about, guys."

Buzz glanced around at the others, to see if anyone was buying it. From the somber expressions all around, it didn't seem like anyone was. But Dex had already gone back up top and closed the hatch behind him.

"Watch out." Vanessa scooted Buzz out of the way as she got up from the table.

"What are you doing?" he asked.

"I'm calling Dad." She stepped over to the navigation station and pulled the black plastic satellite phone out of its wall-mounted charger.

They'd all been shown where it was and how to use it.

"But . . . we're only supposed to use that for emergencies," Jane said. Just then, another powerful gust of wind screeched from outside, tossing the boat into a hard tilt. Vanessa barely caught herself on the countertop to keep from stumbling, while the others struggled to put on their life jackets.

"Yeah, close enough," she said, and started to dial.

Vanessa held on to the nav station desk and sat herself down as the boat continued to tilt and roll. She didn't care if Dexter wanted them using the satellite phone or not. Maybe he'd been through worse, but she sure never had.

The phone wasn't complicated, either. They'd been shown all of the emergency equipment on the first day, when Dex and Joe had taken them through hours of "boat school" before they set sail. Vanessa hadn't paid attention to all of it, but this was something she remembered. She dialed zero-zero-one and then her father's cell number.

As soon as it started to ring on the other end, she felt tears begin to sting the corners of her eyes.

"Hello?" her father's voice came suddenly in her ear.

"Dad?" Vanessa shouted. "Dad!"

"Vanessa, what's going on?" Eric Diaz asked. "I can barely hear you."

"We're in a storm, Daddy. It's bad. Like, really bad."

Jane was there suddenly, reaching for the phone. "Can I talk to Mom? Please? Pretty please?"

Then Carter was there, too. Only Buzz stayed where he was, but he watched just as intently as the other two.

"Where's Dex?" her father asked.

"He and Joe are up top," Vanessa told him.

"Everyone's okay. I'm just . . . I just wanted to hear your voice."

"Listen, sweetie, you're going to be fine. Dex and Joe know what they're doing. Just try to hold on and be brave, okay?"

Vanessa took a deep breath. "Okay," she said, mostly because there wasn't any choice. "Is Beth there, Dad? Jane wants to talk to her."

"All right. Hang on a second. I'll get her."

But before Vanessa could even hand over the phone, an enormous scraping sound screeched up from under the boat. Everything seemed to stop short with a sudden, violent jerk, as if someone had jammed on the brakes. Vanessa felt herself thrown toward the back of the boat. The others tumbled around, too, and the phone flew out of her hand. A cascade of books, dishes, storage baskets, and swiftly unrolling charts came down on top of her where she landed hard against the aft cabin door.

"What just happened?" Carter shouted.

"Did we hit some rocks?" Buzz asked.

"Dad!" Vanessa shouted. "Dad? Can you hear

me?" She started scrambling through the pile of debris on the floor, but she couldn't find the phone anywhere.

Instead, her hand landed in cold water. It was soaking the carpet, Vanessa realized. When she looked to her right, she saw it was also pouring in from under the small engine-compartment door.

At the same moment, Joe came barreling down the galley steps.

"Joe? What's going on?" Vanessa said.

He clambered over the mess as if none of them were even there, and fell onto the wooden stool bolted in front of the nav station.

"What are you doing?" Vanessa asked. "Joe, where's Dex? There's water coming in!"

But Joe wasn't listening. He was holding the sideband radio transmitter with one hand and adjusting a dial on the console with the other.

"SOS, SOS, this is the *Lucky Star*," Joe said into the handset. "SOS, SOS, this is the *Lucky Star*, do you copy?"

Whatever was said next, Vanessa didn't hear. It

was swallowed up by a brilliant flash of lightning and a crash of thunder too overwhelming to be anywhere but right on top of them.

In the next moment, the entire cabin was thrown into darkness.

CHAPTER 3

Buzz's mind was a jumble of panic, fear, and blind confusion. He heard everyone talking at once in the dark, but not what any of them were saying. Jane screamed. Joe was saying something about SOS. Vanessa and Carter were yelling, maybe at each other. The only light in the shifting galley came through the hatchway, from several more flashes of lightning, one after the other.

He was on the ground, somewhere near the back of the boat. That much Buzz knew. It felt like they had crashed, but if that was the case, why were they still moving?

The first thing that made any kind of sense was the stinging chill of water, rising fast around his feet and hands. The shock of it sent him into action, moving faster now than he had in a long time.

He felt his way through the dark, into the rear cabin. It was a small space, so it wasn't hard to find the two tall steps at the back. Struggling to keep his balance, Buzz reached for the place where he knew the companionway door to be. As soon as his fingers landed on the latch, he threw it open and leaned out into the cockpit, where Dexter was holding on to the captain's wheel, trying to steer the boat against the storm.

"What are you doing?" Dex screamed over the wind. "Get below!"

"We can't!" Buzz shouted back. "It's flooding. Water's coming in fast!"

He pointed back the way he'd come. Dexter crouched down to see past him, his headlamp shining inside. When Buzz turned to look for himself, he saw Joe herding the others up the stairs on the opposite side. The water had continued to pour in. It was past Joe's knees already and nearly up to Jane's waist.

Dexter pulled Buzz up onto his feet in the cockpit and slammed the companionway door closed.

"Take the wheel!" he shouted in his ear. There was no question of yes or no. "Hold on as tight as you can. I'll be right back."

"I don't know how to do this!" Buzz shouted. Carter was always the one begging to steer the boat, not him. And now he was supposed to learn in the middle of the world's biggest storm?

"You can do it!" Dex said. "Just hang on!"

"Wait!" Buzz's heart was racing as fast as the wind that whipped past him. There wasn't even time to think. "Where are you going?"

"To open the life raft!" Dex shouted, just before he left. "We're getting off the boat!"

Carter stood at the top of the galley stairs in the

downpour; Jane hovered just behind him, grasping his waist with both hands.

Vanessa was there, too, holding on to the small banister for balance. "Where's Joe going?" she asked.

"I don't know!" Carter said, and leaned farther out to see.

Joe had turned a one-eighty from the stairs and was working his way back toward the middle of the boat where Dex was waiting for him. They quickly started wrestling with the straps that kept the big life-raft capsule lashed to the deck.

Carter felt a cold sense of dread run through him. They were going to have to abandon ship, weren't they? This was even worse than he'd thought.

"Wait here!" Carter shouted at Vanessa and Jane. He clipped himself to the jackline on that side and started to follow back the way Joe had gone. He'd barely taken a few steps before the boat pitched hard again and sent him stumbling to his knees, then flat out on the deck. Even from where he was, though, he could hear the two men shouting at each other over the storm.

"I don't think we can launch in these conditions!" Joe yelled.

"We don't have a choice!" Dex bellowed back.

"But how are we—"

"One of us has to go in with it!"

That was it. There was no more conversation. Within a minute, they'd freed up the capsule. Each of them took a side and heaved the whole thing into the water, where it opened automatically, unfolding and inflating at the same time. Suddenly, there was a bright orange, canopied disc bobbing on the waves—but it was also drifting quickly away from the boat.

"GET IT!" Carter heard Dexter shout. "I'll throw you a line!"

Carter watched from the edge of the deck as Joe dove without any hesitation. He disappeared into the churning water and then resurfaced several yards away. With some effort, he managed to swim over to the raft and scramble up into it.

Working quickly, Dexter had already unspooled an orange floater on a line of rope and tossed it straight out to where Joe was. He wrapped the other end of the line around his own waist, wedged his foot against one of the cleats on the deck, and then motioned for Carter to bring the others over.

When Carter looked back, Vanessa was out on the deck, but she'd clipped herself in on the other side, away from the life raft. And Jane was still peeking around from the stairwell. He couldn't see Buzz at all.

"Come on!" Dex shouted. He held on to the line with one hand and motioned for them to stay low as they came. The boat heeled again to the side, and he stumbled to keep on his feet. "Let's go, let's go!"

"Are we getting off the boat?" Jane yelled when Carter reached her. It was easier to nod than to try and answer right now, and he still needed to get Vanessa and Buzz.

"Hurry!" Dex yelled again. Carter turned to look and caught sight of Buzz somewhere over near the cockpit.

That's when the next crash of lightning hit. Even with the storm raging, it was deafeningly loud.

Carter saw a bright flash from somewhere near the top of the mast, like an explosion of light and force. The sailboat itself twisted nearly all the way around with a violent turn. The life raft veered off in the opposite direction, and Dexter, still holding on to the line, lost his footing altogether. Before Carter could try to get to him, Dex slammed into the railing, flipped over it, and was dragged all the way overboard by the force.

Jane screamed.

"No!" Vanessa shouted.

In a matter of seconds, the boat was driven in one direction and the life raft in another. It was too dark to see clearly, but Carter could just make out the flashing orange light rigged to the raft and the vague glow of Uncle Dexter's headlamp in the water as Joe used the rope line to haul him in. Dex was shouting something back their way, but it was impossible to make out a single word.

Carter stepped onto the rail. He thought about diving in after them, but that seemed like suicide. And he couldn't leave the others. Instead, he looked around desperately for another length of rope or anything he might use to pull Dex back in.

But it was already too late. By the time he looked out toward the water again, Dex, Joe, and the life raft had all disappeared completely into the storm.

CHAPTER 4

Buzz couldn't believe what he'd just seen. It all happened in a matter of seconds. One moment, Dexter was motioning him over to get into the life raft, and the next, he was just . . . gone.

Now the four kids were alone on the sinking boat, left to fend for themselves against the storm.

Buzz stayed low in the cockpit, his arms threaded around the spokes of the captain's wheel. There was no trying to steer anymore. It was only a matter of holding on and trying not to get swept overboard himself.

Heavy sea spray and driving rain smacked

against his face as they crested another enormous swell. The entire boat seemed to stand on end for a moment, its bow pointed at the sky, and Buzz's stomach lurched wildly, just before the hull slammed down hard on the other side.

Keeping to a crouch, he looked around trying to spot the others. Carter and Vanessa were at the front now, hanging on to the rails on either side. Hopefully, they were both still clipped to their safety lines.

But Jane . . . where was Jane? Had she gone over, like Dexter? Buzz scanned the dark ocean all around him—what he could see of it, anyway. Even if he did spot her, he realized, he'd never be able to save her now.

Suddenly, another loud, cracking sound split the air. Not lightning this time. Something even closer. It wasn't until he looked straight up that he realized what it was. The fifty-foot mast towering over his head had begun to sway like a tree about to come down in the storm. And if it did, it was going to fall right toward the two at the front.

"Vanessa! Carter!" he screamed, but the wind seemed to whip the words right out of his mouth before they could do any good.

Next came the sound of popping bolts. Then the groan of metal buckling under its own weight as the mast started to fall.

"LOOK OUT!" Buzz yelled as loudly as he could.

But the storm was louder.

Carter never even heard the mast coming until it crashed onto the deck, just barely to his left. The impact sent him sprawling on his back again. Fiberglass tore like paper around him. Teakwood splintered and broke off at crazy angles. The mast itself dipped, top first, into the water, and then slid right off the boat like a giant goalpost, taking the entire side railing with it.

Before he could even try to move away from the edge of the deck, another wall of water slammed into the *Lucky Star*. It came from the left—port—

this time, sending the boat heeling sharply onto its right side.

Carter grabbed on to the only thing he had left—his safety line. As the boat tipped, gravity took hold, and his body pivoted toward the water. The mesh of the jackline dug hard into his palms, but it held him where he was.

At the same moment, a scream came from across the deck. He looked over—up, really—and saw Vanessa tumbling free of her own line, straight toward him. With the railing gone, there was nothing to keep her from dropping right off the edge and into the water.

Nothing but me, Carter thought, and strained to reach his hand out as far as he could.

Vanessa felt a sharp snap when her safety line gave way. She pinwheeled her arms to try and stop herself, but it was no good. Already, she was falling sideways with the tilt of the boat. Her shoulder pounded hard against . . . something . . . as the world turned upside down and over again in the dark.

The only thing left to grab was Carter's hand. Vanessa reached for it as she went past, and for a moment, they connected. But then her fingers slipped out of his. Her body flew across the last of the rain-slick deck and out over the water.

"Nooo!"

Just as quickly, she snapped back hard. The hood of her raincoat had caught on something, even as the waves below tried to swallow her up to the waist.

"I've got you!" Carter yelled from behind. "Give me your hand!"

Vanessa reached toward his voice, grasping blindly. She found his arm first and started to climb it like a rope, one hand over the other, until she could swing a leg back up onto the deck. She pulled herself the rest of the way on board and collapsed there, catching her breath while Carter clipped her onto his own line.

"Don't move!" he shouted.

Lying flat against the rocking deck of the boat, Vanessa caught sight of Jane huddled on the galley stairs. She was only a shadow in the dark from here, but the tiny size of her was unmistakable.

"Jane!" she yelled. *"Jane!"*

Jane barely moved at all. Her only response was to point back the other way, toward the front of the boat. When Vanessa turned to look, all she saw was a dark blur. But then, with the next flash of lightning, it became clear. The unmistakable, jagged mounds of a rocky shoreline loomed straight ahead of them.

"We're going to crash!" she screamed.

Jane wedged her foot against the opposite wall of the stairwell and squeezed her eyes shut, unable to move or even to yell out. It was like the voice inside her head was trapped there, even as her mouth opened and closed.

Wake up, wake up, wake up!

But this was no dream, and the crash came all too soon.

With one last surge, a huge swell of water rose up under the boat, even as it sent the whole craft hurtling forward. Another unbearable sound of rock tearing at the hull came from below. Jane heard breaking, splintering sounds—and then nothing at all, as the force of the crash sent her tumbling back down into the galley.

She felt herself turning over, and over again, as the water continued to flood into the boat. Then she slammed into something hard as everything came to a fast standstill.

For several bewildering seconds, Jane swung her hands around, trying to find something to grab on to. She couldn't even tell which way was up, and a wave of panic threatened to overwhelm her.

Finally, her feet found solid ground. She stood up quickly, gasping—the water in the cabin was now up to her chest.

But where were the others?

The boat had stopped moving—a bizarre feeling after the roller coaster of the storm—but the wind and rain and lightning were still raging outside as much as ever.

She heard Carter first, shouting her name in the dark.

"Jane? Jane!"

"I'm here!" she screamed back, and stumbled through the water until she hit the galley steps, just as Carter came down to get her.

Vanessa and Buzz were right behind, just shadows in the dark now.

"Are you hurt?" Carter asked.

Jane had banged both her knees, and her head, but nothing felt broken. When she tried to answer, all that came out was a choked sob. Carter pulled her closer and held on tight.

"Hang on, Janie. Don't be afraid," he said. "I've got you."

"What do we do now?" Buzz shouted.

But there was no answer for that, either. The boat seemed to be lodged against whatever rocks they'd landed on, at least for the time being. Everything beyond the edges of the deck was invisible in the dark, and the whole cabin down below was flooded. They were already doing the only thing they could, huddling together on the stairs for warmth, keeping as much out of the storm as possible and just waiting for it to be over.

CHAPTER 5

Carter blinked awake.

At first, nothing made sense. The clean white deck. The bright sunlight. The soft sound of the ocean.

He blinked again, several times, and then remembered where he was. Jane, Buzz, and Vanessa were all right there, still asleep on the stairs. The galley down below was a total wreck, but outside, it was a clear, blue-sky day. Even that seemed strange.

Carter eased his arm from around Jane to crawl up onto the deck and look around. His whole ribcage sent up a sharp wave of pain as he did—from the crash, he remembered. It was all coming back in pieces. When he lifted up his still-damp T-shirt, the bruises on his chest and midsection made him look like he'd gone a couple of rounds with a heavyweight champion.

But he was alive, anyway. They all were. The whole crash seemed like some kind of bad dream now.

Up on the deck, the first thing he saw was the high cliff wall they'd crashed into in the dark. The bow of the boat looked as if it had been chewed right off, leaving the rest of the *Lucky Star* wedged in among the rocks at a shallow angle. It was tricky keeping his footing, but not impossible.

Off to the right, Carter saw where the craggy shoreline continued on for a hundred yards or more before it curved away and out of sight.

To the left, down a short drop from the rocky shelf where they'd landed, was a long stretch of sandy beach. There were palm trees everywhere, and small crabs skittered around the water's edge.

It looked to Carter like somewhere he might want to go on vacation, if he were sitting at home and seeing all this on TV.

But I'm not, he thought. *I am so not.*

Then with a sudden flash of memory, Dexter and Joe came to mind. Carter whipped around to look out at the ocean, instinctively scanning for a flash of orange life raft. He checked the beach again, too, and even looked toward the woods that grew beyond the line of palms higher up on the shoreline.

There was no sign of them anywhere.

"Hello?" he shouted. "Dex? Joe? *Anyone?*"

The only answer that came back was from the other three as they started to stir on the galley stairs.

"Carter?" Vanessa called out.

"What . . .?" Buzz croaked. "Where are we?"

Jane looked up from where she was, wide-eyed and silent.

Slowly, the three of them came up onto the deck. They stayed low at first, as if the boat might start moving again without warning. But in fact, at least thirty yards of rock separated them from the ocean now. The storm's tide had turned around sometime in the night, leaving the *Lucky Star* high and dry.

Nobody said anything at first. Jane came and stuck closer to Carter. Buzz sat down cross-legged on the deck, looking stunned.

"Where are we?" he said.

"Good question," Carter answered.

After another long silence, Jane spoke up next.

"Do you think anyone got that SOS?" she asked, looking at Vanessa.

"I don't know. Probably," Vanessa said. "Maybe."

"Can we try and send another?" Jane asked.

Major duh, Carter thought. That should have been the first thing they thought of. Leave it to Jane. She was the smartest nine-year-old he knew.

Vanessa seemed to agree. Without a word, she'd already turned and run down the galley steps. Everyone else followed closely behind.

Down below, the boat's main cabin looked to Buzz like a disaster area. All the water had drained out by now, but the floor was covered with bloated books, sea charts, cushions, clothing, pots and pans, utensils, and even a few framed maps from the wall, with shattered or missing glass. It reminded him of one of those TV shows where the bad guys come in and trash the good guy's apartment while they're looking for something.

Already, Vanessa had picked her way over to the navigation station, where she was fiddling with several knobs and dials. She was good with computers at home and had spent more time on the boat with all this stuff than the rest of them had. If anyone could figure out how to use the radio, it would be her.

While they all watched silently, she picked up a handheld transmitter that dangled off the console. It was the same one that Joe used to send an SOS the night before.

"Hello?" Vanessa said into the transmitter. "Can anyone hear me? Hello?"

Buzz's heart thudded in his chest, waiting for something—a voice, or even just static. Vanessa flipped several more switches, but it was no good. The radio was clearly dead.

"There's no power," she said. "Buzz, check the engine. Carter, do you know how to try and start it?"

"For sure," Carter said, ducking into the aft cabin and up through the companionway door to the cockpit.

Buzz went to the engine compartment and opened it up. He'd looked in here only once before, and it had been mostly dark. Now, light flooded in where a long, jagged hole had been torn through the hull from the outside. It didn't take an expert to see how badly smashed the engine was. For all he knew, half of it had fallen out through that hole.

"Is anything happening?" Carter yelled down.

"Nothing," Vanessa called back up. "Are you sure you know how to start it up?"

"Yes, I'm sure," Carter snapped.

"Uh, guys? It's not going to happen," Buzz said,

pointing into the compartment. Vanessa came over to look, and then Carter, too, as he climbed back down to join them.

The only thing that seemed to be intact was the electrical bank. It looked like six car batteries, lined up on a shelf at the side of the compartment. Whether they were still hooked up to the rest of the boat, it was hard to say. Even if they were, Dexter had explained on the very first day that there were only two ways to charge those batteries. One was by running the engine. The other was through the boat's solar panel, which was now facedown on the deck, where it had ripped free of its mount during the crash.

"What about the laptop?" Jane asked, picking it up from the mess on the floor. As she did, water drizzled out from several of the ports and even through the keyboard. She tried the On-Off switch anyway, but nothing happened.

"We wouldn't be able to get online even if it was working," Vanessa said. "Not without the modem, and that takes electricity. My cell's around here somewhere, too, but I haven't gotten a signal since we left Hawaii. What we really need is. . . ."

She stopped then, and her hand went up to her mouth. For the first time, Vanessa looked excited.

"What is it?" Buzz asked.

"The sat phone!" she said.

"The what?"

"The satellite phone! I can't believe I didn't think of it before. If it's still charged, we could . . . omigosh! You guys, we could make a call!"

"Well, where is it now?" Carter said.

"I don't know!" Vanessa said. "But it's got to be here somewhere. Everyone . . . start looking!"

Vanessa racked her mind, trying to remember where, exactly, she'd been when she last had the phone. Not that it even mattered. After the crash, it could have wound up anywhere.

"Go through everything!" she told the others.

"Watch out for the glass, though. It's got to be here somewhere."

Soon, they were all picking through the mess and piling it, piece by piece, on the table, the galley counter, and anywhere else they could. It was agonizingly slow going, with so much to sort through. But then—

"Here it is!" Jane shouted. She poked her head out from under the galley table, and held up the chunky black plastic phone. The antenna was up, Vanessa saw, and the small screen above the keypad was lit.

"It's still on!" she said, pressing it to her ear. "Hello? Hello?"

Nobody was there, which wasn't a surprise. It had been at least ten hours since the crash. The question was—how long did these things hold their charge? When she looked at the display again, the green-and-black battery indicator was down to a single bar. But that could be enough.

"Who should we call?" Jane said. Vanessa didn't

have to think about it. She turned the unit off, then on again, and hit the Redial button, just like using a regular phone at home. A few seconds later, it started to ring.

"Please answer, please answer, please answer, please answer. . . ."

"Wait!" Buzz said suddenly. "Shouldn't we try to figure out where we are first so we can tell them?"

The truth of it hit Vanessa like cold water in the face. Of course that made more sense. But then all at once, Beth Benson was there on the phone.

"Hello?" she said frantically. "Dexter, is that you?"

"Beth! It's Vanessa!" she said. All three of the others crowded around, pressing their ears as close as they could get.

"Vanessa! Thank goodness! Is everyone okay?"

"No," Vanessa said. "We're not okay. We crashed, Beth. Is my dad with you?"

"Mom?" Jane called out.

"Jane? Is that you?"

"We're all here," Vanessa told her. "The four of us, anyway."

Beth's voice went up a step. "Where's Dexter?" she said. "Where's Joe?"

"We don't know," Vanessa told her. She heard her own voice crack as she said it, and took a deep breath. It wasn't going to help anyone if she lost it right now. "They were trying to help us into the life raft and it got pulled away before we could get in. Now we aren't sure where they are."

"Vanessa, you're going to be okay," Beth said. "Your dad and I are at the Coast Guard station in Kona. They've been trying to reach the boat all night. I'm going to put you on with one of the people who are going to come help you. Just hold on."

A moment later, an unfamiliar man's voice came on the line.

"Hi, Vanessa, my name's Commander Carl Blakey. I want you to listen carefully, okay?"

There were other voices in the background, too. They were on speakerphone now, and people were listening in. Vanessa imagined a whole room full of them standing there. Somehow, that only made her more nervous.

"Okay," she said. "But, I don't know how long this phone is going to stay charged. There's only one bar left."

"Then let's get right to it," the man said. Vanessa had already forgotten his name. "Where are you on the boat right now?"

"At the nav station," Vanessa told him.

"There should be a GPS unit, either up in the cockpit or right there at the navigation station," the commander said. "It might look like a small TV mounted on the wall, or it could be a handheld unit. Do you know what I'm talking about?"

"I think so," Vanessa said. She remembered Joe saying something about the Global Positioning System on the boat, but right now, she couldn't come up with a picture of it in her mind, and she didn't see anything that looked like a little TV as she scanned the console.

"I'm looking," Vanessa said. "But I'm not sure. Could they have taken it in the life raft with them?"

"That's possible," the commander said. "We never

received any SOS or distress call, so it's been hard to track your location."

Softly, the phone beeped twice in Vanessa's ear. When she pulled it away to look, the battery charge indicator was starting to flash.

"I think the phone's about to run out!" she said.

The commander's voice stayed calm, but he spoke more quickly now. "How about this, Vanessa. Can you tell me anything about where you are? Even just approximately?"

"Find the charts!" Vanessa whispered to the others. All three of them started rooting through the piles they'd just made, pulling out whatever they could find and spreading them on the table.

"Is there anything you remember about your location before the storm?" the commander asked her again.

"Not really . . . I'm sorry," Vanessa said. There were three different charts in front of her by now, but they all looked alike, with their circles, grids, and tiny numbers. "I'm looking, but I can't tell where we are."

Then Jane spoke up. "Boomerang Day!" she said, as if it had just come to her.

"That's right!" Vanessa said. "Right, right! We were just about to come around and head back to Hawaii. That means we were. . . ." She squeezed her eyes shut, trying to remember. "Nine hundred miles from Kona. That's how far we were going. Except then, he started changing course when the weather got bad."

"Your uncle did?" the commander asked her.

"Yes," Vanessa said. "Three times, I think. Or maybe four. We were supposed to—"

Again, the phone beeped twice.

"It's going to run out!" Vanessa said.

"Keep going," the commander told her. "You were supposed to what, Vanessa?"

"We were supposed to get back on course this morning. I know that."

"Which direction? Which way did Dexter alter his course, can you tell me?"

"I don't know!" Vanessa said. The tears were starting to come. She couldn't help it.

"Okay," the commander said. "Okay. Just hold on one second."

"I don't know if I have a second!" Vanessa told him.

And then sure enough, she didn't. There was no last beep, no click, no anything. The line just went dead.

"Hello?" she said. "Hello? Please? Are you there?"

But it was no good. The display on the phone had gone blank, and the people at the other end of the line—including their parents—were gone. All Vanessa could hear now was the wind outside, and the sound of waves breaking softly in the distance.

Vanessa stared at the dead phone in her hand for a long time. She knew there was no way to get the commander back on the line, but that seemed unacceptable. There had to be a way, somehow.

But, of course, there wasn't.

"So, what now?" Carter was the first to say.

"I think we should stay put," Buzz spoke up. "That's what they always say you should do when you're lost, right?"

"We're not at the mall, Buzz," Carter said. "And *they* don't even know where we are."

"We have to find Dexter and Joe," Vanessa interrupted.

Everyone stopped to look at her.

"What do you mean?" Carter said. "How do you even know they're here?"

"They've got to be," Vanessa said.

If they weren't, that meant she was the oldest one here. And *that* meant she was supposed to know what to do. It was one thing to be in charge of the house for a few hours on a Friday night or to watch over Jane while their parents went to a movie. This was something else entirely—as in, life and death.

"They're probably a hundred miles from here by now," Carter insisted. "You didn't see what I saw. That storm blew them away faster than—"

Vanessa cut him off with a glare. "We'll find them," she said.

She knew he wasn't *trying* to scare Jane, but Carter did this kind of thing all the time—talking first and thinking later. Or not thinking at all. She looked him in the eye, then over at Jane, and back again.

"Yeah, okay," he said. "You're right. Let's start looking."

"Um . . ." Jane held up her hand as if they were at school. "I'm thirsty," she said. "Like, super thirsty."

"Actually, me too," Carter said.

"Me three," Buzz said. He was closest to the galley sink and tried the faucet. Nobody was too surprised when nothing came out. The crash had done a lot of damage to the boat.

"There's got to be water somewhere," Vanessa said. "A tank or something."

"There is," Carter said. He was already at the galley table, moving more junk out of the way. "Give me a hand here."

Carter knew exactly what to do next. Uncle Dex had shown them practically everything there was to know about the boat on the first day.

"The water's right there," he said. He went to the U-shaped bench around the table and lifted the long center seat straight off. A large, heavy-duty plastic tank took up most of the space underneath.

"My brother's a genius!" Jane crowed.

"I don't know about that," Carter said, but he liked hearing it all the same. It wasn't that often that someone called him *smart*.

"Okay, genius, how do we get in there?" Vanessa asked.

"It can't be that hard," he said. The tank was meant to be lightweight, for sailing. "We just need something to cut through that plastic. Like a big knife, or—"

"Or an axe," Buzz said. Already, he was unclipping the small axe that hung on the wall next to the fire extinguisher.

"That'll do." Carter grinned as he took it in his hands. This was the kind of thing you'd get yelled at for even thinking about at home. Now there was no choice.

"Be careful," Vanessa said.

"I'll be okay," he told her.

"I meant, be careful with the tank. That's our only water."

Carter nodded. He hadn't thought about that. But if there was one thing he had, it was good aim. He wasn't a two-time Little League all-star pitcher for nothing.

He pointed the tip of the axe blade at the top middle of the big plastic container so he wouldn't miss. Everyone seemed to hold their breath as he raised the axe halfway to his shoulder and brought it down—hard, but not too hard. The corner of the blade punctured the tank on the first swing.

It didn't take long after that. With half a dozen more chops, Carter opened up a triangle-shaped hole big enough to reach through. Soon, they were all dipping cups inside and drinking their fill. Buzz found a dry box of granola bars, too, and they all gobbled those down.

As soon as they had, it was as if everyone's thoughts turned back to Dex and Joe at the same time.

"The sooner we can find them, the sooner we can get out of here," Vanessa said. "Let's get moving."

There were no arguments there. The four of them moved back up the galley steps as a group, ready to step off the deck of the *Lucky Star* for the first time in five days.

CHAPTER 7

The rocky shoreline where they'd crashed looked to Jane like something from an alien planet. As they climbed off the ruined front of the *Lucky Star*, she saw that all the rocks around them were rough, black, and covered with tiny holes. They looked like giant petrified sponges that someone had charred to a crisp.

"I think this is lava," she said. She'd read about this before, how a lot of South Pacific islands had grown out of the ocean from volcanic explosions, over millions of years.

Nobody else seemed interested, though. The idea

right now was to find Dex and Joe. As soon as they'd all jumped from the rocks down to the soft sand below, everyone shed their rain gear and started up the beach, shouting at the tops of their lungs.

"HELLO?"

"DEX?"

"JOE?"

"ANYONE HERE?"

Without talking about it, they spread out as they went. Buzz moved down toward the water's edge. Vanessa stuck closer to the tree line, peering up into the jungle. And Carter and Jane walked straight up the middle of the wide beach.

"Do you think those Coast Guard people will know where we are?" she asked Carter.

"No doubt," he said, sounding sure of himself. "There's probably, like, a hundred people out looking for us right now."

"That's good," Jane said. She hoped it was true, but she'd also seen the way Carter and Vanessa had looked at each other on the boat. Everyone was always trying to protect her, whether she needed it or not.

As the beach started to curve around a bend, Jane stopped and looked back. She was surprised to see how far they'd come already. From here, the *Lucky Star* looked like a broken toy sitting on a stone shelf. The sight of it brought memories of the crash flooding back into her mind, and she couldn't help the tears that started down her cheeks.

As Vanessa and Buzz wandered over, Jane could see Buzz was crying, too. It only made her feel worse.

"What if something terrible happened?" she said with a sob. "What if Dex and Joe aren't . . . coming back?"

Vanessa took Jane by one hand and Buzz by the other. "Everyone sit down," she said. "Right here."

Her dark brown eyes were red around the edges, maybe from the salt air, but maybe from trying not to cry herself. Only Carter looked the same. His jaw was set hard, and his eyes were even harder.

"We're going to find them," Vanessa said. "They'll know what to do. And then they'll do it. I'll bet we'll be on a helicopter before lunchtime." She squeezed Jane's hand. "Okay, Jane?"

Jane nodded. She was glad Vanessa was here right now. She'd been like the big sister Jane had always wanted, even before their parents got married.

"Okay, Buzz?"

"Yeah," he said, and scrubbed his eyes with the backs of his hands.

"Okay, Carter?" Vanessa said.

Carter didn't answer. He was looking back toward the rocky shelf but higher up, above the boat.

"That's totally where we should go," he said.

Jane turned to see. "Where?" she said.

He pointed at a flat rocky outcropping at the top of the cliffs where they'd crashed. From here, it looked like the very ceiling of the island. "I'll bet the view is crazy from up there. That's the place to look for them."

"What do you mean?" Buzz asked. "Like, walk up there, through the jungle?"

"How do you even know you can get there?" Vanessa said.

Carter shrugged. "One way to find out. Who's in?"

Instead of waiting for an answer, he got up and started walking back the way they'd come.

Jane looked at Vanessa to see what she'd do. After a moment's hesitation, Vanessa shrugged, too.

"He's kind of right," she said, and then yelled at Carter's back, "Thanks for waiting!"

Carter didn't even slow down. Their mother always said he was part beagle, the way he liked to be at the front of the pack, no matter what he was doing. In any case, it was better than sitting around crying, Jane thought.

She got up, brushed the sand off her legs, and started following him up the beach. "Come on, you guys," she called back to the other two. "Let's go!"

Carter liked being in the lead. As soon as he'd gotten nearly all the way back to the boat, he looked toward the cliffs to get his bearings, then headed straight up into the jungle.

It was a strange feeling, leaving the beach behind, like moving from one world into another. The trees grew thickly here, in layer after layer of vegetation. Some of them towered over his head, others lay in a random crisscross on the ground, turning the whole forest into one giant obstacle course.

And then there were the mosquitoes—zillions of them, like a tiny army just waiting to attack as soon as someone entered their territory. Carter could hear Vanessa, Jane, and Buzz behind him, slapping at their arms and legs as he led the way.

Not far up the hill, the ground flattened out a bit. As Carter came around a large stone formation, he saw the black hole of a cave, straight ahead.

"Wow," Vanessa said quietly.

"Yeah," Carter agreed. "You could drive a semi truck through there."

The cave's opening was huge and extended farther back than any of them could see.

"Hello?" Carter's voice bounced off the rock walls. "Anyone home?"

"Do you think there are any wild animals around here? Like . . . predators?" Buzz asked tentatively.

"Probably," Jane said. "But not like bears or cougars or anything. More like wild boars."

It was kind of amazing, the way Jane could remember almost everything she ever read. And Jane read a lot. Sometimes Carter called her Chip, because her brain was like one big microchip.

"What's a wild boar?" Buzz said.

"Like a pig," Jane said. "With tusks."

"Oh, like the Minotaurs in Lost Temple 3?"

"I guess."

"Let's keep moving," Vanessa said, slapping another mosquito. "I'm going to run out of blood in a second."

There wasn't anything to see, anyway, so Carter pushed on. Soon, the ground sloped up again, into more woods. Before long, though, several patches of blue sky started to show through the trees overhead.

"I think we're getting there," he said. Straight ahead, he could see a steep, gravelly slope leading up to what looked like another patch of open ground.

"Are you sure this is the right way?" Vanessa asked.

"Totally," Carter said. He wasn't, exactly, but he knew if he admitted it, Vanessa would just try to take over.

He made a running start to get as high up the slope as he could, the shale and gravel sliding away under his feet. Fortunately, there were enough tree roots and larger rocks to give him a few handholds on the way up.

The others came behind. He saw Buzz slide all the way back on his first try, but Vanessa put out a hand to help him up. Jane's small size seemed to work for her, and she made steady progress, keeping low to the ground. She could be a little monkey when she wanted to. At home, she was practically as fast on the climbing wall at their mom's gym as Carter was.

But there was no way Carter was going to let Jane or anyone beat him to the top. He dug his toes into the ground and made it the rest of the way in one last, ragged sprint.

"This way!" he shouted back. "We're almost—AUGH!"

Carter stopped short, pinwheeling his arms to keep from falling over the edge of a sheer drop-off. It had only just shown itself as he reached the summit. His stomach flip-flopped, and he took a quick step back, kneeling down to steady himself on the ground.

"What is it?" Vanessa called up.

"Be careful," he shouted. "There's, like, a gorge or something up here."

What was in front of him now was a deep ravine that seemed to split the island's cliffs right in half. All he saw way down at the bottom was a jumble of brush and more rocks.

And straight across, Carter could see the rocky outcropping he'd spotted from the beach—so close now but completely beyond their reach.

CHAPTER 8

By the time Buzz got to the top of the gravel slope, Carter, Jane, and Vanessa already had a plan for what to do next. So much for taking a break and catching his breath.

"We're going to head over there," Carter said, pointing along the edge of the ravine.

Maybe fifty feet to the right, there was a stand of tall trees clumped together. One of them had come down—recently, from the look of it. Now it stretched across the gap like a natural bridge.

Buzz looked down into the ravine. It was like looking off the roof of a ten-story building, and it gave him a hollow feeling in the pit of his stomach.

"You want to cross that thing?" Buzz said.

"Do you see a better way?" Carter asked. Already, they were on the move, hiking laterally along the edge of the chasm.

It didn't take long to reach the base of the tree. Dirt clods hung off the exposed roots, and the leaves on the branches at the far side were still green.

"I bet it came down in that storm last night," Jane said. She looked nervous but ready to go.

Buzz took a deep breath. "Shouldn't we vote on this or something?" he said.

"What is it with you guys and voting?" Carter asked.

"That's what we always used to do at home," Vanessa told him. She meant before their parents had married each other. "Like when we'd rent a movie and couldn't decide what to watch."

"Yeah, well, we'd just rent both movies. That way, everyone gets what they want," Carter said. "I'm not turning around now."

"I think I'm going, too," Vanessa said, and put a

hand on Buzz's shoulder. "You don't have to come if you don't want. You can keep watch."

Buzz was already dripping with sweat, but he felt his face go a little warmer still. *Keep watch?* that was what the popular kids always told the fat kid when they didn't want him around. And he wasn't even that fat.

"I'm coming," he said before he could think about it too much. "Just . . . go."

Carter went first and climbed right up through the roots to stand at the very base of the trunk. The whole tree was huge, at least three feet thick.

"Feels solid to me," he said. Then he dropped onto his belly, straddled the trunk with his legs, and started pulling himself across.

Buzz watched what he did, trying to memorize every move. The only time he'd done anything even close to this, it had been with a game controller, an avatar, and a couple of spare lives.

He couldn't help feeling a little jealous of Carter. This kind of stuff was always so easy for him. In about three seconds, it seemed, Carter had made it across and was dropping to the ground on the far side.

"No sweat!" he shouted back. "Come on!"

Jane scrambled up next and started right across. Once she was out of earshot, Vanessa turned to Buzz.

"You really don't have to," she said.

"I know," he answered. But he was still going to do it. There were probably worse ways to die—not that he could think of any right now.

As soon as Jane had made it across, Buzz gritted his teeth and climbed up onto the base of the trunk.

"Stay low," Vanessa said softly. "And don't look down."

"Stay low. Don't look down," he repeated.

"And keep moving."

Buzz nodded, took one more deep breath, and then inched his way out over the edge of the ravine. This was like a platform game, only real. There was nothing to be afraid of, right?

"Nothing to be afraid of," he muttered to himself. "Nothing to be afraid of. Nothing to be—"

That's when he looked down. The only thing between him and the rocky bottom was ten stories of empty air. His stomach swooped, and his heart started thumping even faster. One false move, he knew, and he was boulder meat.

That's why you don't look down, Buzz thought.

"Keep going!" Vanessa yelled somewhere behind him. Always the cheerleader, his sister.

"Okay," he mumbled again. "Okay, okay, okay. I can do this."

He reached out, got a grip on the trunk in front of him, and pulled himself a little farther along. Then he did it again. And then again.

By the time he'd found a rhythm, Buzz realized he was more than halfway across. The far side of the ravine had somehow become the near side.

"You got it!" Vanessa shouted.

A few more pulls and he found himself climbing down through the fallen tree's branches to where Carter and Jane were waiting for him. In a weird way, the whole thing had gone by quickly, like a fast nightmare.

"See?" Jane said. "It wasn't that bad, was it?"

"Nah," Buzz said, playing it off. The truth was, he felt incredible—and incredibly relieved.

"Right here!" Carter reached out and gave him a rare high five. "You did it."

"Yeah," Buzz said.

"That was the hard part. Going back will be cake."

"Yeah . . . wait, what?"

Buzz realized he hadn't even thought about that. This was not a one-way trip. He was going to have to crawl back across that tree if he wanted to get back to the *Lucky Star*.

Still, there was nothing to do about it now. He was going to enjoy some solid ground for a while and worry about everything else later.

Either that, or the rescue plane could just pick him up here when it came.

As soon as Vanessa reached the others on the far side of the tree bridge, they all continued on together, up toward the rocky point Carter had spotted from the beach down below.

Coming out onto the open ground of the summit, the view was almost exactly what she'd expected—like a whole world of water spread out around them.

Straight down, she could see the *Lucky Star* where it sat, ruined on the rocks. And behind them, as Vanessa turned all the way around, the shape of the island itself came clear for the first time.

The whole thing was a giant ring of land, encircling an enormous lagoon of the most brilliant aqua-blue water Vanessa had ever seen.

"It's just a big circle," Buzz said.

"It's called an atoll," Jane told them. "That circle used to be the top of a volcano. Now it's sinking back into the ocean."

"How fast?" Buzz asked cautiously.

"Not that fast," Jane said.

The ridge where they were standing seemed to be the tallest and widest part of the island. As the land arced around, it thinned out into a green and sandy-brown strip on the opposite side, divided in several places by bright blue stripes of water. From here, that part of the island looked like giant stepping-stones.

The other thing that had become painfully clear was just how empty the ocean was, all around them. There was no sign of any other land. No sign of civilization, for that matter.

And worst of all—no sign of Dex and Joe.

"Anyone see them?" Vanessa asked. When nobody answered, it was like something breaking into a million pieces. She hadn't realized how much she'd been counting on finding them until it became clear that it wasn't going to happen. Now it seemed like she'd been fooling herself all along.

"Maybe they're in the woods or something," Jane said. "And we just can't see them."

"Maybe," Vanessa said, but she didn't believe it. She'd heard what Carter said earlier. That life raft had been blown clear away from the boat in seconds, and it hadn't been traveling toward the island. Besides, if Dex and Joe were here, they would have found the *Lucky Star* by now, wouldn't they? The island wasn't *that* big.

"Sorry, guys," Carter said. "I guess we came all the way up here for nothing."

"It's not your fault," Vanessa said.

"I didn't say it was my fault," he started up.

"Relax," she said. She'd already had enough of Carter for one day. "I was just saying—"

But then it was Buzz who interrupted them.

"Actually," he said, "there is one other thing we could do."

CHAPTER 9

Suddenly, Buzz had everyone looking at him. He even almost forgot what he was going to say for a second.

"We need to build a signal fire," he told the others.

"A what?" Vanessa said.

"I've seen it on TV. You know, those shows where they drop some guy off in the middle of nowhere and he has to survive by himself?"

Carter looked over at him. "You watch survival shows?"

"I watch a lot of stuff," he said.

That's where his nickname had come from.

His father was the first to use it, because he said that Benjamin was always watching something or playing some game that went *crash*, *bang*, or *buzz*.

Buzz didn't mind. It was better than being called Benjamin, for that matter. Jane and Carter had only ever known him as Buzz, and that was just fine with him.

"The first thing those TV guys always do is build a fire, somewhere up high," he went on.

"Like right here," Jane said.

"Yeah. That way, if a plane or a boat comes around—"

"*When* a plane or a boat comes around," Vanessa interrupted.

"Okay. *When* that happens, we're going to be way too small to see. But a fire with a bunch of smoke can get their attention."

Carter was nodding the whole time and even seemed kind of impressed. "Boy, you do watch a lot of TV, don't you?"

Everyone seemed to be into the idea, so Buzz kept on talking.

"We're going to need some stuff from the boat," he said. "Like one of those signal flares in the cockpit and some rope."

Dexter had made them all go through hours of safety drills before they left Hawaii, and the coolest part of that training was, by far, the emergency flares. When you pulled the cap off the top of a flare, it self-ignited into a super-intense mini-torch. On the ocean, they were for visual signaling, but you could also use them to set almost anything on fire.

"I'll go," Carter said right away. "I'm the fastest."

"Of course you are," Vanessa said.

That sounded good to Buzz. "And get that axe, too," he said. "We're going to need to chop up some big branches."

Carter took off like he was in some kind of race, while Jane, Vanessa, and Buzz started collecting materials. It felt good, but also kind of weird, to see everyone doing exactly what he told them to do. Buzz wasn't usually the boss of anything in their family, especially not with Vanessa and Carter around.

"We need a bunch of really dry grass," he told the girls. "And then some little twigs, and then dry branches on top of that."

The fire was going to have to be tall, he knew, with room at the bottom for air to circulate. The bigger the stack, the bigger their signal would be when they set it on fire, and the better their chances of being spotted from far away.

Jane ran around and found an amazing amount of stuff to put at the base—dry grass, sticks, and even some papery tree bark. Buzz had seen the TV guys use coconut husks before, but the only coconut trees they'd seen so far were all down at the beach.

Carter was right about being fast, too. He got back with everything they needed just in time to start using the axe. He and Vanessa were also the strongest, so they took turns with it while the others carried twigs and dead branches over to where Buzz was putting it all together in a pile.

It was slow going. A few times, the whole structure collapsed in on itself and Buzz had to start over. At home, with a pitcher of lemonade or even just some shade, it might not have been so hard. But out here in the open sun, it felt like he'd sweated about eight gallons by the time it was done.

Just as the sun was heading down toward the horizon, the group put on some finishing touches. First, they wrapped the stack in the biggest, darkest palm fronds they could find. That was something else Buzz had remembered—that green leaves made bright white smoke when they burned, the kind that was easy to see from a distance.

After that, Carter cut up some pieces of rope with the axe, and they tied the whole thing up so the wind wouldn't take it apart while they were gone. Last, Buzz stuck the emergency flare all the way inside, at the base of the structure, for safekeeping. He hoped he could be the one to set it ablaze when the time came.

"There," he said, and stood back to look at what they'd done. "We're all set."

Now all they needed was a boat. Or a plane. Or a helicopter. Or anything at all to get them off this stupid island.

By the time they were all back down at the beach and climbing up onto the deck of the boat, Carter had exactly two things on his mind: food and water.

"I'm staaaarving!" he said. "What do we have to eat?"

They all moved straight down the stairs into the galley to start looking for whatever they could find. It was getting dark now, but Vanessa found a flashlight in the nav station, and that helped.

"Hey, look—marshmallows!" Buzz said.

"We've got some cans of beef stew," Vanessa said. "Chili. Ravioli. Fruit cocktail."

"I'll fill some cups," Carter told them, and went straight for the water. He pulled away the bench seat covering the tank, picked up a coffee mug from the table, and dipped it down in through the hole he'd cut that morning.

But instead of water, all Carter found inside was air.

"Hey!" he shouted. "Where'd it go?"

"Where'd what go?" Vanessa said.

"The water!" he said. "It's just . . . gone."

"It can't be," she said, coming over with the flashlight. She shone it inside the tank, then didn't say anything for a long time.

"What do you see?" Jane finally asked.

Vanessa sat down slowly. "He's right. There's a big crack all along the bottom. And one of these pipes is hanging off."

The news settled silently over the group.

"Maybe it broke when we cut it open with that axe," Buzz said.

"Don't blame it on me!" Carter told him.

"I'm not," he said. "I'm just saying what might have happened."

Vanessa slammed her fist against the table. "We shouldn't have been gone so long!" she said. "If we'd been here, we would have noticed, and we might have been able to do something about it."

Still, it felt a whole lot like blame to Carter. He also felt like he was suddenly three times thirstier than he'd been even a minute ago.

"What else is there to drink?" he said.

Jane and Buzz were already on it. They were opening cabinets and looking in the little refrigerator, but so far, they didn't have anything.

"One gallon of nasty-smelling milk," Buzz said, taking it out. "And . . . not much else. Some carrots and a bunch of D batteries."

"What about outside? It's not like we aren't surrounded by water," Carter said.

"You can't drink seawater," Jane said. "It's so salty, it just makes you thirstier. Or sick. I forget which. Maybe both."

"There were a bunch of juice boxes before. And some soda," Vanessa said. "I'm positive."

"We finished the soda on the second day," Buzz said.

It was true. Dex had made a big deal about bringing soda at all, since it was so heavy and took up a lot of room. The juice boxes at least were lighter and you could crush them up when they were empty. But that also meant they could have easily been washed away in the crash and the flood.

Carter looked around. A lot of provisions had been lost. He felt ready to start tearing the boat apart, piece by piece. He'd never cared about stupid juice boxes before, but he would have traded his BMX bike for just one of them right now.

This was unbelievable. The longer the day went on, the worse it got. The whole thing was starting to seem like the world's stupidest problem. Who got *shipwrecked* anymore? Dex was supposed to watch out for them. And where was he now?

"How could they just leave us on our own like that?" he blurted out.

"Who?" Vanessa said. "Dex and Joe?"

"Yes, Dex and Joe!"

"They didn't do it on purpose," Buzz said. "It was just an accident."

But Carter didn't want to hear it, especially not from Buzz, sitting there with his bag of marshmallows like this was some kind of camping trip.

"You're not much help, either," he said. "Where were you when the boat crashed last night?"

"I was trying to steer!" Buzz yelled back at him.

"Yeah. 'Trying.' Exactly," he said. "And when you were crashing the boat, I was saving your sister from going overboard!"

He was starting to say stuff he knew he shouldn't. But sometimes it was hard to stop once he got going.

"Vanessa's your sister now, too," Jane told Carter.

"Yeah," Buzz said. "And it wasn't me who crashed the stupid boat!"

"Have another *marshmallow*, Buzz." Carter felt ready to hit something, or explode, or both. It seemed like everyone was ganging up on him, even Jane.

"Don't talk to him like that," Vanessa said. "And stop acting like a little kid. You want to have a temper tantrum? Go do it somewhere else."

He glared over at her. She wanted him to go somewhere else? Fine with him. His mother was always telling him to count to ten when he got mad. So he counted his steps—right out of the galley and up onto the deck. When he got to the bow of the boat, he just kept going, onto the rocks, then down to the beach.

That's when he started running. Vanessa and the others were calling after him, but he didn't care. He just needed to get away, as fast and as far as he could.

He was crying now, too. Like a baby. He hadn't cried all day, not even once. But he couldn't hold back anymore. The tears just kept coming, streaking across his cheeks as he sprinted farther and farther up the beach. At least there wasn't anyone to see it.

Finally, he couldn't run anymore. His knees buckled as he rolled to a stop right there in the sand, panting and catching his breath. And thinking about the others.

Sometimes, he wasn't sure why he got so mad. He just did. One thing piled on top of the next, and then he lashed out. Usually at Buzz—he was too easy a target. But this wasn't Buzz's fault, he knew. It wasn't anyone's fault. It was just bad luck, the same as he'd been having all year long.

A week ago, it seemed like his biggest problem

was moving away from his old house, changing schools, and dealing with Vanessa's know-it-all attitude 24/7. Now all of that seemed like a joke in comparison to being stranded in the middle of nowhere.

There were no adults here to help, and someone had to take charge. There was so much they needed to do. They needed to find water if they were going to last. They needed to start keeping watch for rescue planes. They needed—

A sudden, loud rustling noise from the woods pulled Carter right out of his thoughts.

His heart jumped back up to full speed as he listened. Something was there. Something big, from the sound of it. He heard twigs breaking and underbrush being pushed aside.

In fact, it wasn't just one thing, he realized. It was a group of them. A group of . . . *something*. And they were right there, maybe twenty feet away, in the woods.

Carter stayed low in the sand and as still as possible. What was it Jane had said about wild animals? He couldn't remember. He hadn't really been listening, but now he wished he had.

The next sound he heard was a soft snorting—or a sniffing, like maybe one of them had just picked up his scent. Almost right away, the others joined in.

Without a weapon, or even a flashlight, Carter started to feel like a giant target, sitting there in the dark. Who knew how many of them there were? How outnumbered he might be? Maybe this place was full of predators—or whatever they were—roaming the island at night.

As the rustling in the woods grew louder, and then closer, one clear thought rose above the rest: *Time to go.*

The words went off in his mind like a starter pistol. Carter sprang to his feet, ducked his chin, and ran. He didn't look over his shoulder once. He just sprinted all the way back to the boat like his life depended on it. Which maybe it did, and maybe it didn't.

But this was no place to take chances.

CHAPTER 10

"Hi, everyone, it's Jane B. again, reporting for Evanston Elementary."

Jane stood on the rocks next to the *Lucky Star*, holding her camera out in front of her. The sun was just coming up, and the others were all still asleep. But she'd been awake for hours, scratching her bug bites and trying not to think about how thirsty she was.

It was a surprise when she'd found the camera in one piece after the crash. Jane knew it was waterproof, but apparently, this one was shipwreck-proof, too. The battery still had most of its charge, so there was plenty of time to work on her report, if she wanted.

"Today is June thirtieth, and it was supposed to be the sixth day of our trip," she continued. "I kind of skipped a day yesterday, but let me show you why."

She moved the camera sideways now, to take in the huge hole in the side of the boat. It looked like a giant had taken a bite right out of it.

"That's the boat we were sailing on, until we crashed here," she said. "We don't even know where we are, exactly. I'm just calling it Nowhere Island for now. These rocks where I'm standing are Dead Man's Shelf. And up there . . ."

She leaned way back to show the place at the top of the cliffs where they'd built the signal fire.

"That's Lookout Point. Oh, and over here is Benson-Diaz Beach. See?"

The names were just something she'd thought up lying in her bunk, wide awake most of the night. Later, if she could find some dry paper and a pen, she'd start making a real map, too.

"Jane? What are you doing down there?" Vanessa

called out from the deck. She'd just come outside, still looking sleepy, but her dark hair was pulled neatly off her face in a short ponytail, and she'd put on clean shorts and a T-shirt. She looked ready for business.

For some reason, Jane felt embarrassed. "I was just working on my report," she said.

Vanessa gave her a look, the same one adults did sometimes. It was a confused sort of smile, like maybe Jane was too smart for her own good.

"You can work on that later," she said. "Come on up. I want to have a family meeting."

"About what?" Jane asked.

Vanessa shrugged, like it should be obvious.

"Everything," she said.

In the cockpit of the *Lucky Star*, Vanessa set out the last can of fruit cocktail, half a bag of marshmallows, and four spoons. There was still a full jar of peanut butter and some canned chili and beef stew they could eat, but for now it seemed like a good idea to stay away from anything that might make them even thirstier.

"Why do we have to have a family meeting?" Carter wanted to know right away.

"Because we have to figure out what to do today, and who's going to do it," Vanessa said.

"We don't need a meeting for that. We can talk while we're looking for water. That's, like, the world's biggest *duh* to me."

You're a big duh, Vanessa thought. But she held her tongue. There had been enough fighting the night before. Carter hadn't said a word when he came back to the boat, but he'd obviously been crying.

Now she couldn't help thinking about what her dad would say about all this. *Work it out*. Every time there was a disagreement in the new house—about computer time or who got which bedroom or whether someone had taken something that wasn't theirs—it was always the same: *You don't have to love everything about one another, but you do have to figure out how to get along. We're one family now, not two.*

So work it out.

"We definitely need water," Vanessa agreed. "But I've been thinking about that solar panel, too." She pointed over to where the broken panel was sitting facedown on the deck. "If we can get the satellite phone charged up again, we could make another call."

Carter looked at her like she was speaking Russian. "Are you serious? When was the last time you hooked up a solar panel?"

"Never," she told him. "But I'm good with stuff like that."

"It's true," Buzz said. "She is."

It wasn't like she knew for a fact that she could do it, but it was worth a shot. The back of the panel had only a few wires sticking out of it. Maybe it wouldn't be that hard.

"Uh, hello? Is anyone besides me really thirsty?" Carter asked.

"We don't need four people to look for water,"

Vanessa pointed out. "We can get more done if we split up."

"I think we should stick together," Jane said.

"I think we should stop talking about everything and start doing it," Carter said.

"Hey, and where are we supposed to go number two, anyway?" Buzz asked. Vanessa felt like she was ready to scream. This meeting was going downhill fast.

"Come on, you guys," she said. "We have to make some decisions. Let's just take a vote, okay?"

But Carter was already on his feet. "I vote I'm going to look for water so we don't all die of dehydration. Jane, you can come with me if you want."

Jane looked at Vanessa.

"Fine," Vanessa said. In fact, she realized, they both wanted the same things, anyway: water, rescue, and a little time apart from one another.

So much for their family meeting.

"Let's just get to work," she said.

CHAPTER 11

Carter pulled the straps of his backpack a little tighter. Jane had one, too. Both of them were filled with as many jars and bottles as they'd been able to find on the boat. With any luck, all those containers would be full by the time they got back.

"Remember, stick to the beach," Vanessa called after them. "That way, you can't get lost."

She was just trying to help, Carter knew, but sometimes Vanessa sounded more like a mom than his mom did.

In fact, it had been Jane's idea to walk around the outside of the ring-shaped island. If there was fresh water here, it would flow downhill toward the ocean. With any luck, they'd cross paths with it along the way.

They headed off in the same direction as the day before, away from the crash site.

For the first long stretch of beach, Jane seemed fine. She'd even brought her camera and made some of her little videos while they walked. But then the land started to curve off to the right, and they quickly lost sight of the *Lucky Star* behind them. That's when Jane started getting nervous.

"I still think we should have stuck together," she said, looking back.

"Don't worry about it," Carter said. "Vanessa's right. We don't need four people to do this. But don't tell her I said that."

It was supposed to be a joke, though Jane didn't even smile. Instead, she started asking questions. That's what his sister did when she was anxious—she gathered information.

"How big do you think the island is?" she said.

"I don't know. Maybe five miles around," Carter told her.

"How long does it take to go a mile?"

"It depends. The world record is under four minutes, but that's on a track."

"Carter? What if we don't find any water?"

"We will," he said.

"How do you know?" Jane said.

Carter stopped walking. "Look around," he told her. "Half this island is green. There has to be water somewhere."

That seemed to satisfy her. Carter even felt a little proud of himself for thinking of it so fast.

But then she asked, "How long do you think this is going to take?"

That one was trickier. There was no way of knowing, but that seemed like the wrong thing to say.

"Not too long," he told her as casually as he could, then continued on up the beach.

It would be several hours before either of them

realized just how wrong Carter had been. But by then, it was going to be too late to do anything about it.

Vanessa stood on the deck, looking at the solar panel like some kind of giant puzzle. The glass surface was in a million pieces, but the inside still looked intact.

Maybe Carter was right. Maybe she was crazy to think she could ever do this. But she had to try.

"Help me lift this," she told Buzz. The panel wasn't heavy, but it was big and awkward. They each took a side and slid it up onto the cabin roof. Then they climbed up next to it and propped the whole thing against the metal bracket where it had lived before the crash.

Hopefully, this first part wasn't going to be super complicated. The back of the panel had one white wire and one black wire sticking out of it. Likewise, the electrical box on the mounting bracket had one white wire and one black wire, all of them with exposed copper ends where they'd torn free.

Vanessa looked across at Buzz. "White to white and black to black, right? That makes sense."

"I guess," he said. "Like that lamp Dad fixed a few weeks ago."

"Right." She remembered now. Anytime she'd seen their father do anything like this, the colors always matched up.

As she bent down to take a closer look, Buzz spoke up again, quietly this time.

"What do you think Dad's doing right now?" he asked her.

Vanessa didn't have to think about that one. "Looking for us," she said. "I'll bet he and Beth are on some Coast Guard plane right now, flying around up there."

When she looked at the sky, the clouds had started to roll in overhead. That was bad news. Even if they did get this panel hooked up correctly, they'd have to wait for the sun to come back before they could test it.

"Vanessa?"

"Yeah?"

"What happens if they can't find us?"

"I don't know, Buzz," Vanessa told him honestly. "We've still got the boat. There's still a bunch of food. Hopefully, Jane and Carter are going to find water. We'll just—"

"Just *what*?" Buzz was looking her right in the eye now. He didn't just want to know, she could tell. He *needed* to know.

"We'll work it out," she said. "Okay?"

That actually made him smile. "That's what Dad would say." She smiled, too.

"Now come on, let's do this," she said, and knelt down next to the panel.

There wasn't any electricity running on the boat, so there didn't seem to be any danger of getting electrocuted. Still, Vanessa was careful. She used a pair of rubber-handled pliers from the cockpit to twist the two white wires together, nice and tight. After that, Buzz had to lift the panel up so she could slide underneath it, like a car mechanic, and do the same thing with the black wires.

As soon as it was done, they both ran down to the main cabin. The batteries in the engine compartment looked like they were hooked up, but there was no way of knowing for sure. The console at the nav station still looked just as dead and blank as ever.

That was no real surprise. Until the sun came back, they wouldn't know if they'd made any progress here. Even then, they were going to need the satellite phone charger to work. And even *then*, they'd have to try and figure out where in the world they were so they'd have something to say if they finally got to make another call.

That was a lot of ifs and a lot of maybes, Vanessa knew. A total long shot. But an hour ago, they'd had no chance of reaching the outside world at all. Now they did.

And a long shot was way better than no shot at all.

"YES!"

Jane looked up from tying her sneaker. Carter was walking in a small circle now, and he spiked an imaginary football over his shoulder.

"What is it?" Jane said.

"Over there! See?"

They'd been hiking for hours, with no luck, and the land around them had started to thin out. As the wall of the jungle dropped away behind them, they'd gotten their first look at the island's huge inner lagoon from ground level. Jane had seen the lagoon from above, on Lookout Point, but not the cliffs that faced it on this side.

The cliff walls themselves were dotted all over with dozens of black holes—more caves, Jane realized. Some were just small openings, but others were at least as big as the one they'd found in the woods on the opposite side of the island.

"Do you see it?" Carter said.

"See what?" Jane said.

"Give me your camera."

He took it and zoomed in on the cliff wall, directly across the lagoon from where they were standing. As the image came clear, Jane swallowed hard—or, at least, she tried to. Her throat was sore and as dry as paper.

But right there on the camera's view screen was a small waterfall. It spilled out of one of the caves from a height of about ten feet. The water cascaded over a rock formation into a pool down below, then continued on toward the lagoon.

Carter grinned. "I told you we'd find it. Come on!"

Jane didn't need any coaxing. She was exhausted

from the hike, but the sight of the falls got her moving again. It was too far to swim all the way across the lagoon, so they continued around it, in the same clockwise direction they'd been going.

Soon, they were at the very narrowest part of the island. The ground was just sand and beach grass here, with several small streams cutting across their path as they went. It was like a chain of tiny, sandy islands, one after the other.

The first water crossings were easy. They barely slowed down as they splashed right through. But then they came to a much deeper channel.

"Keep going," Carter said. "Hold my hand."

As they started to cross, it only took a few steps before the water was up to Jane's chin. The current was stronger than she'd thought, and her feet left the ground a few times before Carter pulled her back close. By the time they'd reached the next patch of dry sand, both of them were soaked and out of breath. Jane's wet pack felt twice as heavy as before.

"I hope that was it," she said.

But it wasn't. They'd barely scaled the next dune before Jane realized their luck was running out. What stretched in front of them now was something like a fast-flowing river, from the ocean to the lagoon.

"I think we have to go back," Jane said.

"I don't think we can," Carter told her. For the first time, he looked truly worried.

When Jane turned around, she saw why. The last channel they'd managed to cross was now just as high as the one in front of them. The tide was rushing in and their tiny island was shrinking by the minute.

"We're going to have to swim across," Carter said.

"It's too fast!" she said.

Jane was a good swimmer; she'd been doing it all her life. But that was in pools and in Lake Michigan back home. Here, there was nothing to stop her from getting carried off like a piece of driftwood.

"I'll check it out first," Carter said. "Then I'll come back for you."

"No, don't!" Jane said.

The only thing worse than being stuck here together would be if they got separated. She grabbed for Carter's arm, but it was like trying to stop a bulldozer.

He walked straight into the channel up to his waist, then dove away.

Carter was shocked at how quickly the current took him. The moment his feet left the ground, he felt himself swept sideways, away from the direction he wanted to go.

"Carter!" he heard Jane yelling, but there was nothing he could do now.

Immediately, he knew he'd made a mistake. He turned over in the water, trying to stroke his way back to shore. But it was too late for that. Before he could take another gulp of air, he felt himself tumbled back underwater by the current.

His pack wasn't helping, either. The straps bound him up as he tried to swim. The more he struggled, the more he felt wrapped up like a mummy, unable to move his arms at all. He had to get free of it or he'd drown.

Carter bucked and jerked with everything he had, struggling to ditch the pack. His lungs burned, desperate for oxygen that wasn't there. What he got instead was a giant gulp of salt water.

Finally, with a last desperate twist, he pulled one arm loose, and then the other. There was no thought of trying to keep the pack anymore. All his mind could perceive was the need to breathe, and he kicked toward the light at the surface of the water.

Just when it seemed as if his lungs were going to pop in his chest, Carter broke through, hacking up water and sucking down air practically at the same time.

"Carter!" Jane yelled somewhere behind him.

He spun around in the water toward her voice. That's when he realized just how far from the sandbar he'd been carried. Jane was a good hundred yards away. She'd dropped her pack but was standing in the channel up to her knees now.

"Jane!" he croaked out. His throat burned from the salt water. "Stay right there!"

She seemed to hear his voice but not what he was saying. Instead of staying put, Jane took another cautious step forward—and that was all it took. Carter saw his sister go down as the water swept her right off her feet.

After that, he couldn't see her at all.

CHAPTER 13

Buzz stood on the deck of the *Lucky Star*, scanning the beach with a pair of cracked binoculars. Carter and Jane had been gone all morning and now a good part of the afternoon as well. So far, there was no sign of them.

No water, either. The inside of his mouth felt like paste on paste.

"Hey, Vanessa?" he called down. "Don't you think they should have been back by now?"

"I don't know," she said. "This is Carter we're talking about. He won't be able to show his face unless he finds water."

It was true, Buzz thought. Carter was stubborn that way.

Still, it was hard not to worry. Once you'd gotten shipwrecked in the middle of nowhere, it was pretty easy to imagine other bad things happening, too.

"Maybe we should go look," he said. "Just walk up the beach or something?"

"If they're not back in an hour, we'll start looking," Vanessa said as she came up the galley steps. "But come here. Check this out."

She was carrying a spiral-bound book of maps in her hand, and she laid it open on the deck to show him. Buzz crouched down to have a look.

The map in front of him was a two-page spread with the title "Islands of Oceania" across the top. It showed the west coast of the United States in one corner, Australia in the other, and a wide expanse of Pacific Ocean in between.

"So, we set sail from here, six days ago," she said, putting her finger down over the big island of Hawaii. On the map, it was about the size of a Skittle. "And when we left, I'm pretty sure we sailed south and west."

She drew a diagonal line with her finger, past something called Johnston Atoll, then out into the biggest empty space of ocean on the page.

"This is about nine hundred miles from Hawaii," she said. "That's how far we were supposed to come. I don't know how much farther that storm blew us, or which way Dexter changed course, but I think we're somewhere around here."

Buzz felt a quickening inside him. They knew where they were! This seemed like it could be big—except . . . He glanced at his sister and saw the furrow between her eyebrows. Why wasn't Vanessa more excited?

The nearest land to where she'd pointed was the Marshall Islands to the northwest, then something called U.S. Kiribati to the southeast.

"What's U.S. Kee-ree . . . batty?" Buzz asked.

"It doesn't matter," she answered impatiently. "What I'm saying is, this whole area is about fifteen hundred miles across. And we're *somewhere* in the middle of it."

He looked back at the map again. Fifteen hundred miles was Chicago to California. Half of the United States.

"So, even if the Coast Guard is looking for us . . ."

Vanessa nodded. "It's like the biggest, worst game of hide-and-seek, ever."

"And we aren't even trying to hide," Buzz said.

The reality of it settled over him like a dark cloud. All day long, he'd been thinking about rescue. Hoping for it. Relying on it. Now it was starting to look like they might be stuck here for a lot longer than he'd imagined.

Buzz stood up and re-scanned the empty beach. Even though Vanessa had said not to worry about Carter and Jane, that didn't really seem possible anymore.

"Vanessa?" he said.

"Yeah . . . okay," she said. She already knew what he was thinking. "We can start looking for them right now."

Carter's heart leaped when he finally spotted Jane in the water. The current had her in its grip, carrying her right toward him.

"Jane!" he yelled, but she didn't seem to hear. She was struggling to swim, her head just barely above the surface of the water.

Carter stroked against the tide with everything he had. The most he could try for was to keep from drifting farther away, as Jane washed in his direction. It was like swimming upstream, and his arms weren't going to cut it much longer.

The next glimpse he got of her, she was less than twenty yards away and closing in fast—but just off to the side.

On instinct, Carter stopped trying to swim. He stretched his arms and legs into a wide X-shape instead, as much like a net as he could make himself. Jane was there now, and she caught his eye.

"Carter!" she yelled again. "Help me!"

They collided in the water and Carter grabbed hold. He flipped onto his back now, keeping his grip on Jane. His arms were too weak to swim against the tide anymore, but he could still kick. So could she.

"Turn over!" he yelled. With a fast scramble, they were hooked arm to arm, like one unit. "Now kick!" he said. "As hard as you can!"

The water at their feet roiled as they started to flutter and kick and inch their way back toward the shore. It was slow going, but they generated enough power to keep moving in the right direction. Carter aimed them for the middle of the sandbar, where the current was weakest.

Finally, the water grew shallow enough that he could see the lagoon's sandy bottom. "We've got it!" he said. He reached down with one foot, then the other, and found he could stand.

Jane was even more exhausted than he was. He wrapped her arms around his neck and her legs around his middle. Then he trudged them both back up onto the tiny island's shore.

As soon as he had dry sand under his feet, Carter collapsed onto his knees. A bellyful of salt water came up and burned his throat all over again. His vision blurred and fuzzed.

Jane rolled off him and lay on her back, panting.

"Are you okay?" he said.

She just nodded. There were no words right now, for either of them. Carter knew that this could have turned out even worse than it did. In a way, they'd been lucky.

After several minutes, he stood up again and looked around. The water was still rushing in from the ocean. As long as that was the case, they weren't going anywhere.

"How long does it take for the tide to turn around?" Carter asked. It seemed like something Jane would know.

"Maybe six hours?" she said. "But . . . I think that might be too late."

She was looking at the sky now, as if there were some answer up there. All Carter could see overhead was a solid gray sheet of clouds.

"Too late for what?" he said. He almost didn't want to hear her answer.

"For us," she said. "The tide has to go down sometime, but so does the sun. And I've got a bad feeling about which is going to happen first."

CHAPTER 14

Vanessa nearly cried when the rain first started. It came after hours of walking the shore of Nowhere Island, looking for some sign of Carter and Jane. She and Buzz stopped long enough to stand on the beach with their mouths open, letting the drops moisten their dry tongues and throats. It wasn't much, but the relief was intense.

Soon, they were up in the woods, where rain had started to gather on the thick foliage. It was Buzz's idea, something he'd seen on one of his shows. If someone had told her a month earlier that she was going to be licking plants for water, Vanessa would have thought they were crazy. Now the only thing that was crazy was how good it felt to lap up a tiny bit of moisture from a waxy green leaf in the middle of the jungle.

Still, the good feelings didn't last long. As darkness set in, there was no choice but to head back to the boat. They'd missed their chance for Lookout Point, too. Even if they could get through the jungle at night, they wouldn't be able to see anything until morning.

"We'll go first thing," Vanessa said. "We'll find them, Buzz. I promise."

Buzz only nodded. This seemed to be weighing even more heavily on him than it was on her. And the hard truth was, they were still going to have to worry about water no matter what happened. That meant collecting as much of this rain as they could, right away.

As soon as they reached the *Lucky Star*, Vanessa went straight downstairs to grab whatever containers she could find. She pulled a cooking pot and a frying pan out of the galley, set them up on the deck, and then ran down for more.

"Buzz? Where are you? What are you doing?" she yelled. There was no knowing how long this rain would last.

When she came back up with a flashlight and an armful of cracked coffee mugs, Buzz was standing on the cabin roof. He was trying to free what was left of the torn mainsail from what was left of the broken boom.

"Help me get this off," he said. "We can tie it across the deck and catch water with it."

Vanessa looked at her baby brother. It was a brilliant idea. One she never would have thought of. She set down the mugs and jumped up next to him. They worked as quickly as they could, untying lengths of cord and cutting through knots with a steak knife from down below. By the time they'd freed up the sail, they had an enormous parachute-sized piece of material to work with.

"Over here," Buzz said. "Quick."

Following his lead, Vanessa helped stretch the sail across the back of the boat. They tied it to the rail on two sides and to the captain's wheel in the cockpit. When they were done, the whole thing hung loosely over the deck like a giant cloth bowl. A small pool had already started to collect in the center.

"Buzz, you're some kind of genius," Vanessa said, standing with him in the pouring rain. "Did you see that on TV, too?"

"No," Buzz said.

"Some video game?"

Buzz shook his head. "It was just something I thought of," he said.

It seemed like he didn't want to talk about it. Vanessa felt pretty sure that he was already back to thinking about Carter and Jane. Back to worrying, too.

Still, she couldn't help noticing that Buzz was adapting to all of this faster than anyone. Maybe he was going to surprise them all before it was over.

In fact, he already had.

Jane shivered in the dark as the rain poured down on their little sandbar.

It didn't matter if the tide had gone out now or not. Without any moonlight or even starlight to navigate by, there was no way to leave. The darkness was complete here, like the definition of pitch black.

At first, the rain was a good thing. They'd lain flat on their backs, catching what they could in their mouths and in some of the jars they'd brought. She still had her pack, but Carter's was gone. They only had half as many containers as when they started.

Now, hours later, the rain was just one more torment to deal with. If Jane had wondered how things could get worse since the crash, this was her answer.

"What time do you think it is?" she asked Carter.

"I dunno," Carter answered dully. It was the same voice he used whenever one of his teams lost a game.

"I think the sun comes up around six," she said.

"Whatever," he answered, and hunched his shoulders a little tighter.

Besides everything else—the hunger, the rain,

the darkness—Jane was also chilled to the bone. She and Carter huddled together on the sand for warmth, and she tried to use her empty pack as a blanket, but none of it did any good. Their one lucky break was that the water had stopped rising before it swallowed their tiny island completely.

"Carter?"

"What?"

"Do you think Vanessa and Buzz are out looking for us?"

"They'd be stupid if they were," he said. "They should just wait until we come back tomorrow."

Jane hugged herself and tried to stop shivering. "Do you think it's at least midnight by now?" she said.

"I don't want to talk about what time it is."

"Okay."

Instead, she shut her eyes and thought about that word, *tomorrow*. Hopefully, the sun would come up extra-extra early in the morning. She imagined it, rising over the cliffs and shining warmly down on her face.

Then slowly, the image faded and another one took its place. She saw her mother and Eric now. They were standing on the front porch of the house, waving at her to run up the sidewalk and come inside.

That part was the hardest of all—thinking about home. Their kitchen full of food. Her warm bed. Her friends. All of it was five thousand impossible miles away. Even getting a hug from her mother right now would have been like winning some kind of big prize.

But still, Jane was determined not to cry. Not in front of Carter. At least, not until she saw the sun again. Then she could do whatever she wanted, she told herself.

In the meantime, she just had to hang on.

Buzz took the first watch that night. He let Vanessa get some sleep and stood on the deck in his raincoat, watching the dark beach.

He kept the flashlight, too. He pointed it up the shore and clicked the button—on, off, on, off, on, off. Every minute or so, he repeated the pattern. The beam didn't reach far, but it was something Carter and Jane could follow if they were trying to get back this way.

It was also something Buzz could do. He had a terrible, helpless feeling in his gut, wondering where they'd gone. It kept reminding him of what Jane had said that morning.

I think we should stick together.

Now he wished more than anything that he'd listened. They all should have. Maybe Jane was the littlest, but she was probably the smartest one in the group. Because right now, letting those two go off by themselves felt like the stupidest mistake they could have possibly made.

CHAPTER 15

Carter woke up scratching.

Somewhere in the night, the rain had stopped and the bugs had moved in to take its place. Even as he sat up, he was waving away a cloud of them. When he looked at his arms and legs, they were lit up with dozens of small red welts. Maybe hundreds. And every single one of them was itchy.

It was the first night any of them had slept outside, Carter realized. Just one more reason why he couldn't wait to get back to the *Lucky Star*.

And that's where there was some good news. In the early-morning light, he could see that the water had finally gone down. Their sandbar had grown overnight, and had even reattached itself to the larger curve of the island. They were free to go.

"Jane, wake up," he said. He was already on his feet, still scratching as he put all the bottles and jars back into her pack.

"What happened? You look like you have the measles," she said. Her own arms and legs were nothing compared to his.

"I guess I taste better to mosquitoes," he said, shouldering the pack. "At least someone got to eat last night."

It had been over thirty-six hours since they'd had anything besides rainwater, he realized. The inside of his belly felt like it was grinding against itself. His steps weren't as sure-footed anymore, and his head swam a little as they set out. The hike back to the boat was going to be rough, but he tried not to think about it. If Jane could do this without complaining, then so could he.

Slowly and steadily, they came around the curve of the lagoon toward the falls. Neither of them had the energy to run, but they did pick up their pace as they came within striking distance.

The falls themselves spilled out of a cave opening, about ten feet off the ground. The water flowed over a jumble of rocks and into a small pool, which fed into the lagoon. With one last burst of adrenaline, Carter and Jane splashed right through the little pool to stand at the base of the falls. The water was ice cold, but Carter let it spill right over him. It felt amazing on his burning skin, and then even more amazing to finally drink his fill.

It wasn't exactly the chocolate-chip-pancake breakfast with bacon and sausage, scrambled eggs, and everything else he'd been dreaming about all night. But for right now, it would have to do.

As soon as Jane had enough to drink, her thoughts turned to the cave where this water was coming from. In fact, she'd been thinking about it all night. And she'd begun to wonder if maybe . . . just maybe . . .

"Carter? What do you think is up there?"

"What do you mean?" he said, wiping his mouth.

"Well, if we could drill a hole straight through this cliff, how close to our beach do you think we'd come out?"

Carter shrugged. He never had any patience for the little mind puzzles she liked so much.

"What are you talking about?" he said.

She pointed up at the cave again. "Where do you think that goes?"

Now Carter seemed to get her drift. "I don't know. Maybe nowhere," he said. "Where do *you* think it goes?"

"I'm not sure," Jane said. "But . . . maybe somewhere."

It was worth checking, anyway. They'd spent the whole previous day getting this far around the island. If they could find a way through, it would be the world's best shortcut.

She let Carter climb first, as they headed up the rocks along the side of the falls. It was harder to concentrate on an empty stomach, so she took her time and followed Carter's steps from one foothold to the next.

As she scrambled up over the lip of the cave, cool air rushed out to greet her. It felt air-conditioned inside, and her wet skin prickled with goose bumps.

Jane took a few steps farther in. It was hard to see very far before the darkness took over. The ground sloped up from here, and a fast-moving stream ran down the middle of the rock floor, on its way to the falls.

"Jane, I don't know about this." Carter sounded wary.

"No, this is perfect. We can follow the water," Jane said. "Then, if we think we're lost, we can just follow it right back here again."

"I wish we had the flashlight," Carter said. The ground underfoot was uneven and hard to see even near the mouth of the cave.

But that's when Jane remembered her waterproof camera.

"Maybe we do," she said. She turned Carter around and unzipped the front pocket on the pack.

Then she took out the camera and switched it on.

The battery charge was down to about half by now. Hopefully, that would be enough. She flipped it over to play mode and pressed the Start button.

> *"Hi, everyone, this is Jane B. again. Today is July first, and we're out here looking for water . . ."*

As her most recent journal entry played, the view screen lit up with a small glow. In the dark of the cave, it was just enough to show Jane the ground in front of her, if she held it low enough.

"Nice!" Carter said. She felt a high five whiff past her ear. "You want me to go first?"

"I'll do it," Jane told him. The idea of leading the way into this pitch-dark hole was scary, but she kind of liked it, too. She'd never led Carter *anywhere*.

"Come on," she said. "Stay close."

CHAPTER 16

Please, please, please . . . oh, please.

Vanessa stood on Lookout Point, silently begging for some sign of Carter and Jane to show itself. It had been almost twenty-four hours now. Wasn't that when you were supposed to call the police?

But, of course, that wasn't going to happen. They were on their own here.

"You see anything?" Buzz asked.

"Nothing," she said. The shore was empty, and the jungle was too thick to see into from up here. She kicked at the ground in frustration. "They could be anywhere in those woods. I told Carter to stick to the beach, but he's so stubborn, he probably went tromping around in there just because I said not to."

"We should keep moving," Buzz said. They'd been on the point for at least half an hour now. "If they're not back at the boat when we get there, I think we should start walking again. All the way around the island if we have to."

Vanessa nodded, but she was also torn. She hated to leave this spot. At the same time, she hated to think that Carter and Jane could be hurt and waiting for them to come help. Maybe she and Buzz should split up to cover more ground. Or maybe that was the worst idea in the world.

There were no perfect answers for this. Not even any good ones.

The cave led uphill into the dark and quickly banked to the right. Soon after that, Carter couldn't see any light behind them at all. The only thing they had to go by was the six inches or so that Jane's camera lit up in front of them.

"It couldn't have just been a straight shot, could it?" Carter grumbled. " 'Cause that would have been too easy, right?"

"What was that?" Jane said, stopping all at once. Carter brushed something away from his head as it flitted past. Or, at least, he could have sworn he felt something. Already, the dark was playing tricks on them.

"Any way we can go faster?" he said.

"Not really," Jane said. The stream was still on their right, and he could hear another waterfall up ahead. The sound had been muted at first, but it was getting louder with every step.

"Watch out for this," Jane said. They'd just come to a low wall of some kind. Carter kept one hand on her arm and felt his way along with the other as they climbed up to stand on a higher elevation.

They'd just come into a much bigger space, from the sound of it. Everything was more echoey here, including the falls, which were somewhere off to the side.

In front of them, in the camera's light, Carter could see the edge of a pond or a pool of some kind. It was impossible to know how big it was, but it was feeding the stream they'd followed inside. The falls he heard seemed to be flowing down into the same pool. That meant the water was coming from somewhere even higher up.

It was easy to imagine the whole cavern as some kind of crazy, multilevel maze—the kind you walked into and never came back out of. The thought of it put a shiver down his back.

And right now, they had a big decision to make.

"Which way?" Jane said. With the pool in front of them, there was no more stream to follow, or to lead them back if they got lost.

Just then, something else whizzed past Carter's ear. A bug or a bat or . . . something.

"Let's just keep moving," he said right away.

"Follow the edge of the water. We can always track it back to the stream, right?"

"Yeah . . ." Jane said tentatively. "Unless there's a whole bunch of streams. How will we know which one to come back to?"

It was a good question. Getting lost would be a pretty stupid move, Carter thought. But then again, turning around might be, too, if they were getting close.

And standing still in the pitch dark was starting to drive him crazy.

"I say we go for it," he told her.

Buzz still didn't love crossing the tree bridge, but Carter had been right. The first time was the hardest. And Vanessa was right, too. It helped if he stayed low, kept moving, and most of all, didn't look down.

The rest of the way to the beach was familiar by now, and easy. They slid down the gravel slope on their butts, using their heels to brake as they got near the bottom. Then they continued on around the giant rock formation and started past the mouth of the cave in the woods, before the ground began another downward slope.

It was quiet as they walked. Neither of them seemed to have much to say. But then, as they passed the cave, Buzz thought he heard Vanessa mutter something under her breath.

"What?" he asked.

"Huh?" Vanessa said.

"What did you just say?" he asked her again.

"I didn't say anything. What did you hear?"

Buzz stopped to listen.

"Nothing, I guess," he said.

And then—there it was again. Some kind of mumble.

He and Vanessa stared at each other, wide-eyed. She'd heard it, too. It was coming from the cave. The hairs on the back of Buzz's neck stood up. Was it a wild animal? One of those boars Jane talked about?

"Hello?" Vanessa called out.

And then, a small voice came back. "Hey! Vanessa? Is that you?"

It was Carter . . . somehow. Buzz felt more shock than relief at first. None of it made any sense, almost as if they were hearing things.

Both of them rushed in through the mouth of the cave, as much as they could. The daylight from the woods behind them didn't reach very far. Soon, Buzz was facing a wall of blackness he didn't know how to navigate.

"Carter? Jane?" he yelled. "Are you in here?"

"Keep talking!" Carter called out. "Where are you?"

It was hard to know how to answer that one. "We're . . . here!" Buzz yelled. "Where are *you*?"

He could feel Vanessa's hand on his shoulder behind him. "Should we get the flashlight?" she said. "It's still on the boat."

"I don't know," Buzz answered.

Then he saw it for the first time—a faint, tiny glow just coming around some unseen corner in the dark. That's all it was at first, until Jane called out again.

"There they are!" she said. "Omigosh . . . it really is . . . Carter, we did it! We're back!"

Before Carter could stop Vanessa, she had her arms around him, in a big hug.

"I'm so glad to see you!" she said. He could barely breathe, she was squeezing so tight. "I never should have let you go off like that!"

Carter's first thought was, *What do you mean, let us?* But this was too happy a moment to worry about that right now.

"Okay, okay," he said, stepping back. He was glad to see them, too, but there didn't need to be a whole production about it.

It was hard to believe, but Jane's idea had actually worked. If it weren't for her, they would have spent the whole day hiking back to the boat on empty stomachs.

"Where did you come from?" Buzz asked, peering into the dark.

"From the other side," Jane said excitedly. "These cliffs are like Swiss cheese. There are caves everywhere."

"And we found water, too," Carter said. "There's a falls back there. At the lagoon."

"It's called Carter's Falls," Jane said with a grin. "You could get there in two minutes with a real flashlight."

For everything they'd been through, she seemed pretty pumped, Carter thought. And pretty tough, for a nine-year-old.

"But, I don't understand," Vanessa said. "Are you guys okay? Why didn't you come back last night? What happened?"

"We're okay," Carter said. Already, he was heading toward the mouth of the cave ahead of the others. "Let's talk about all that on the boat, because I'm staaaarving!"

CHAPTER 17

Lunch was a celebration—two cans of ravioli, one of beef stew, one of chili, and four spoons.

"Cheers!" Jane said, holding hers up. She'd never thought she'd be so glad to eat cold ravioli.

"Cheers!" everyone said, and they clinked cans right before they all dug in. It felt good to be back together, like a real family. And now, between Carter's Falls and the rainwater Vanessa and Buzz had collected, they could get as thirsty as they wanted. There was plenty to drink.

While they ate, Carter and Jane told the whole story of what had happened to them. Then Vanessa and Buzz told about Buzz's sail rig for catching water and the solar panel they'd put in place.

"Maybe it's all hooked up, and maybe it isn't. I just don't know," Vanessa said. "We need some sun to find out for sure. This weather's driving me crazy."

It was just starting to rain again, and Jane could hear thunder rumbling in the distance. It looked like the weather was going to get worse before it got better, but she didn't even care. At least they were inside the boat this time.

And they were making progress, too. It was exciting to think that they might actually be able to use the satellite phone again. Maybe even in the next day or so. She couldn't wait to talk to Mom and Eric.

When they were done eating, it was time to get back to work. Vanessa and Carter spent most of the afternoon going over every inch of cable they could track, from the solar panel to the engine compartment and over to the nav station, trying to make sure everything was good to go.

Buzz worked on organizing all of their provisions and bottling up the rainwater he was collecting in the mainsail.

And Jane did some investigating of her own. Vanessa had already started to figure out their location on a map, but not in a way that was going to help them tell the Coast Guard where to look.

There were lots of navigation materials in the cabin down below. Most of them had been scattered around in the crash, then piled into one corner or another. Some of the sea charts were on the table, others were rolled up in the nav station. There was also a huge stack of books on the floor by the rear cabin door. Jane started digging through them, and that's where she found Uncle Dexter's captain's log.

It was a tan clothbound book with an image of a jumping swordfish on the cover. Whether Vanessa had been through this stack or not, Jane didn't know. But the log grabbed her attention right away.

Inside, Dex had filled page after page with his small, sloppy handwriting. There were dozens of sketches and diagrams, too. He'd dated every entry, going back for three years. It was kind of like looking at Dex's homework.

As Jane flipped through, she saw drawings of dolphins and whales; descriptions of places Dexter had been to, like Samoa and Fiji; and tons of notations about latitude, longitude, and other words she didn't even recognize.

At the back, on the very last written page, Jane found an entry marked for 10:00 a.m. on June 28—the day of the big storm.

> *Got a cold front coming in, faster and slipperier than I thought it was going to be. Heading into some tricky water to try and get around this storm. The kids seem kind of nervous, but they're troupers.*

Jane stopped there and stared at the page. She wondered if Dex and Joe were still out on that life raft somewhere. It had been three whole days now. Did they have water? Food? Could they fish?

Had they been rescued? She hoped so, for everyone's sake. If there was anyone who could tell the Coast Guard where to look for Nowhere Island, it would be them.

She looked down at the journal again. She'd seen Dex scribbling in it before, a little bit every day, when he worked on navigation with Joe. Usually, they'd look at the charts in the morning, then he'd write in his log while Joe steered the boat. She'd even gotten a little of that on camera for her report.

And that's when it hit Jane. Maybe, just maybe, there was something she'd recorded that they could use.

She ran back to her bunk and got her camera off the shelf where she kept it. Then she sat right down on the cabin floor and started looking.

It didn't take long. Within a few minutes, she found the exact entry she'd been thinking about.

> "Hi, everyone, it's Jane B., and today is June twenty-seventh. It's the third day of our sailing trip, and today, I'm going to show you how navigation works. . . ."

Jane's heart sped up right along with the video

as she pressed Fast Forward. When Dexter came onto the screen, she let it play again.

"So you see, this is the sea chart we're looking at today," Dex's voice said over the tiny speaker.

As he unrolled the chart, she pressed Pause. Looking as hard as she could, it was still impossible to pick out any real details on the view screen. It was too small. But then, when she hit Play again, Dexter picked up a pencil and circled something several times.

> "This is a coral reef. That's something we want to make sure and work our way around. . . ."

Again, she froze the image. She jumped up and ran over to the galley table, starting to flip through every chart she could find.

Vanessa and Carter were peering into the engine compartment as she did, and they looked over now.

"Jane? What are you doing?" Vanessa asked.

"I think I may have figured something out," she said. "I was just looking at one of my videos—"

"You should really save the batteries on that thing," Vanessa said.

"Don't worry about that," Jane said, pulling out another chart.

And there it was—the ragged circle of pencil from before. She looked back at the camera's screen one more time to be sure.

Yes. It was the same circle. The same chart.

"This is where we were, just before the storm," she said, pointing.

"How do you know?" Carter asked. Buzz was just coming belowdecks now, too, and they all crowded around.

Slowly, Jane told them everything that she'd just figured out. Vanessa looked at the chart, then compared it to a map she'd found in a spiral-bound book.

"Okay . . ." she said excitedly. "Okay . . . we might be closer to . . . here." She put her finger down on the chart. "Five hundred miles northeast of the Marshall Islands. At least I think so."

"There's this, too," Jane said, holding up Dexter's

journal. "We might be able to find out more about which way we came."

The others were all looking at her now, smiling a little with their eyebrows raised. She'd seen that look before, in school. It happened every time she answered a problem one of her teachers thought nobody would ever get.

Nobody but Jane Benson, that is.

CHAPTER 18

Vanessa couldn't sleep. She lay on her bunk across from Jane, staring at the dark ceiling of their cabin and listening to the rain pound down outside.

Instead of getting any sun before the end of the day, they'd only gotten more and more rain. More wind. More thunder and lightning. It was beyond frustrating, when the sun was the one thing they needed most at this point.

As she lay there with nothing to do but think, Vanessa realized she was also starting to hear a new sound from outside. Something that hadn't been part of the mix before.

It was almost like a washing machine, sloshing clothes around and around. The noise came, then stopped, then came again.

What is that? she thought.

The next time, it was twice as loud—not just a soft splashing, but more like a watery crash against the side of the boat. She'd heard that sound before, she realized, on the worst night of her life.

The flashlight was on a sill next to her bed, where she'd left it. She grabbed it now and stood up. The wind was kicking around outside, along with the rain beating against the cabin roof. Vanessa took her slicker off the hook by the galley hatch and zipped it up tight around her. With the bad weather, the temperature had dropped considerably.

A downpour hit her in the face as she slid back the hatch. It felt like sharp little droplets, stinging her cheeks and making it hard to look around.

Keeping as low as she could, she came off the galley stairs and shone the flashlight back toward the rear of the boat, past the cockpit. What she saw took her breath away.

It was almost as if they were at sea again. The ocean had advanced on their rocky shelf, and deep water was pooled all around them. Before Vanessa could even make sense of that fact, a heavy wave rolled in from out of the dark and broke hard against the back of the *Lucky Star* in a burst of sea spray. The sight of it shocked her into action.

She scrambled back down the stairs, not even bothering to close the hatch this time.

"You guys!" she shouted. "Wake up! Right now!"

She went to Jane first and pulled the blankets off her, shaking her awake. Then she went to the boys' bunks, where Carter was stirring and Buzz was already sitting up.

"What's going on?" Buzz asked.

"Get up! There's water all around us," Vanessa told them. "I think we have to get off the boat before it's too late."

"What?" Carter was wide awake now, too.

"Get whatever you can," Vanessa said. "But fast."

"Are you sure?" Jane said, standing close now, right behind her.

Before Vanessa could answer, there was another rushing, watery sound all up and down the side of the boat. For the first time since the crash, the *Lucky Star* moved. It rose out of the tilt where it had been for the last several days, listed up and over, and then came down hard on its other side with a resounding thud.

"Yeah," Vanessa said, starting to gather up whatever was closest to grab. "I'm sure. Now move!"

Carter's mind raced. His pack was long gone, somewhere in the middle of the lagoon, so he pulled the case off his pillow and started grabbing what he could. If they were getting off the boat, this might be his only chance to save a few things. And they were going to need all they could get.

"Vanessa! We need the flashlight!"

"Get out here!" she screamed from the galley. "We'll take what we can."

Buzz had balled up their two blankets and got

out the door ahead of Carter, though Carter was right behind.

Water was pouring in from both ends now, and it sloshed around their feet. It reminded Carter that he wanted his shoes, but when he looked back, the cabin was clearly too dark to try and find anything in there.

Vanessa was gathering something from the nav station. Jane had her own pack and was pulling what she could from the galley. With everything in shadow, it was hard to see or know what to do or what to grab. The first thing Carter recognized in the dark was the axe. He stuffed it head down inside his pillowcase pack.

Again, a wave broke outside the boat. Again, the *Lucky Star* lifted and floated free for just a moment before it slammed down hard against the rocks. Carter heard the hull cracking, as it had on the night of the crash. His heart pounded. There was no knowing how much time they had left—but it didn't seem like much.

"We have to go!" he said.

"I know!" Vanessa yelled. "Come on."

Buzz was throwing what he could up onto the deck, while Carter wrapped his arms around the pile of charts and books on the galley table. There was no seeing which was which in the dark. All of that was secondary right now. He stuffed what he had into the pillowcase and let the rest drop to the ground, forgotten.

Then he grabbed Jane by the arm and pushed her up the galley stairs.

Then Buzz, then Vanessa.

Carter was the last one out.

Jane stood on the deck, trying to take in what was all around them. Vanessa was up ahead with the flashlight, shining it off the bow of the boat. She motioned the rest of them over and pointed down toward the beach.

"We need to time this right!" she shouted. The waves were rushing in to hit the cliff wall in front of them, then pulling back, then rushing in again. It explained how the *Lucky Star* had gotten this far up Dead Man's Shelf to begin with. But Jane also realized that the boat wasn't going to stay there for much longer. Each wave sent it shuddering back and forth now, almost as if it were restless and ready to go.

Jane felt Carter's hand on her shoulder again, urging her up toward the bow. When the boat tipped suddenly to the side, both of them fell to the deck. They stayed down and crawled to where Vanessa was waiting for them.

"Buzz!" she shouted as they got there. Jane looked back, and he was bringing up the rear, his arms filled with whatever he had grabbed.

Carter left her there with Vanessa and went to help him up the slippery deck.

"Ready?" Vanessa shouted in her ear. "We're going to jump after the next wave comes."

"We have to wait for them!" Jane said, looking over her shoulder. They couldn't leave the boys alone on the ship.

"They're coming!" Vanessa shouted. "Let's go."

Jane was just as terrified of staying as she was of jumping. They'd done it in the daylight with no problem, but not like this. Never like this.

Still, there was no choice. She locked arms with Vanessa and shut her eyes as the next explosion of water hit the cliff wall in front of them, then pulled back.

"Now!" Vanessa said.

Blindly, she jumped and hit Dead Man's Shelf, just a few feet below. Her grip left Vanessa's, but only for a moment. They found each other again and scrabbled together, over the rocks and toward the beach. Jane could feel the sharp edges cutting into her hands, but it was hard to care about that right now. When they reached the drop-off, they jumped again, this time onto wet sand.

"Keep moving!" Vanessa said. She pulled Jane along, up toward the woods. Jane could hear the scraping sound of the boat over the rocks. And she could only hope that the boys were right behind her, too.

Buzz and Carter reached the edge of the deck at the same time. With the bundle in his arms, it was hard for Buzz to see ahead, but he was going to hold on tight to everything he had for as long as he could.

"Come on! We can do this!" Carter yelled. There was no time to think. "Ready? One, two, three!"

They jumped onto the rocks and continued in the same direction Vanessa and Jane had just gone. A few moments later, they were down on the sand, looking around for the girls.

"Up here!" Vanessa shouted from somewhere just inside the tree line. He saw them then, huddled under a low-hanging palm. Vanessa gestured them over, while the rain continued to beat down.

"Is everyone okay?" Carter asked as soon as they were all together again. Buzz nodded. He was as okay as he could be, considering.

The next thing they heard was the crash of another wave, and then a long, loud scraping sound, different from the ones before. He leaned out to see back toward the beach and the rocks. Vanessa shone the flashlight that way, just in time to show them the *Lucky Star* as it was washed away from its former resting place and back out toward the ocean. It was like watching a house get swept away. In fact, it *was* their house.

However far the boat got, Buzz couldn't see. It slipped beyond the edge of the flashlight beam with one last groaning, splintering sound, and disappeared.

When he looked around at the other three, each of them was just a shadow in the dark.

"What are we going to do now?" Buzz asked.

"The cave!" Jane shouted.

It was a good idea. The cave was farther uphill but not too far to reach. It would at least let them get out of the storm until they could make sense of everything that had just happened.

There was no need for any more conversation. All four of them turned at the same time, holding on to one another as they pressed up into the woods behind Vanessa's flashlight beam.

“Stick together!” Buzz shouted. He’d never meant anything more in his life. Everything they thought they had going for them had just been washed away, back into the ocean.

All they really had now was one another.

CASTAWAYS FOUND ADRIFT AT SEA—FOUR STILL MISSING

KONA, HAWAII—A sea captain and his first mate were rescued early this morning, adrift in the life raft that was meant to save all six people on board their sinking boat.

Captain Dexter Kingson and First Mate Joc Kahali, both of Kona, Hawaii, spent the last four days with only emergency rations as the swiftly moving southerly Pacific currents swept their small raft farther and farther from the site where Captain Kingson's boat, the *Lucky Star*, ran aground of a rocky shoal on the night of June 29.

Also on board the *Lucky Star* were four young passengers—Vanessa Diaz, 13; Benjamin Diaz, 11; Carter Benson, 11; and Jane Benson, 9. Coast Guard representatives in Kona have confirmed hearing from the children, but communication was lost before a specific location could be determined.

Search and rescue operations are working with Captain Kingson and Mr. Kahali, trying to re-create the life raft's drift since it was separated from the *Lucky Star*, but recent weather conditions, combined with seasonal wind and water currents, have frustrated their efforts. The search continues daily.

ACKNOWLEDGMENTS

I'd like to thank anyone, anywhere, who had anything to do with making this project happen. And, because writers are supposed to be specific, I'll add a few names here:

Thank you to sailors extraordinaire Jill Kuramoto, P. Milo Frawley, and Sam Culver for sharing their knowledge and experience with us. This adventure never could have left port without them. The same goes for Tom Champlin and Carl Elwert at Alteris Renewables, who taught me a thing or two (or three) about solar power.

Thanks also to some of my favorite *Survivor* survivors—Kathy O'Brien, Cirie Fields, Rob Mariano, and Amber Brkich—as well as Dr. Liza Siegel, for their unique insight on what it means to be a castaway.

This story also benefited from some good ideas, careful reading, and friendly encouragement along the way—starting with Paul Lasher, Angela

Galyean, and their amazingly thoughtful students at Hinesburg Community School. It also included early-draft readers Jan Donley, Barbara Gregorich, Vicki Hayes, and Joe Nusbaum, who shone a light on the good, the bad, and the in-between. Kyle Jablonski could always be counted on for a great idea in a pinch. And Jonathan Radigan is—and always has been—the muse with the mostest.

Thanks also to George Nicholson and Caitlin McDonald at Sterling Lord Literistic, and to copy editor Sandy Smith and to Abigail Powers and Pat Shuldiner at Puffin for their eagle eyes.

And lastly, a big double down ditto on all of the above, with thanks to our editor at Puffin, Jennifer Bonnell, who is as patient and insightful as she is great to work with and good at what she does.

—CT

THE ADVENTURE CONTINUES IN

They thought it couldn't get any worse. They were wrong. Being shipwrecked on a jungle island was bad enough. But now that Carter, Vanessa, Buzz, and Jane have lost their boat to another storm, it's like starting over. Survival is no individual sport in a place like this, but there's only one way to learn that. The hard way.

CHAPTER 1

Vanessa forced herself to take another step. Then another. And another. It was everything she could do to keep from dropping to her knees in the mud and giving up. But that was the last thing any of them could afford.

It was the second huge storm in a week. The first had crashed their fifty-foot sailboat, the *Lucky Star,* onto the rocky shore of this tiny island. Now another one had come along and dragged the boat—their only shelter—back out to sea. The four of them had been lucky to get off alive as they'd scrambled over the rocks, onto the beach, and up into the jungle.

"Keep moving! And stay together!" she shouted to the others. Her voice was already hoarse, trying to be heard over the wind, and thunder, and crashing waves. She held her flashlight out in front of her, but it was hard to see. The rain poured down in sheets, even under the jungle's thick canopy of trees.

They moved in a tight clump, holding on to one another and to the few things they'd managed to take. Jane and Buzz stayed close on either side. Carter was right behind, pushing the group to go faster. Behind them, Vanessa could hear the tide pounding the shore, each wave a little higher than the one before it. If they didn't keep heading uphill, it was going to be one of them who got washed away next.

"I think I dropped something!" Jane called.

"Leave it!" Vanessa told her. "Don't stop!"

"But—"

"I said leave it!"

She didn't like yelling at Jane, even now, but it couldn't be helped. The only thing that mattered was finding shelter. And that meant getting to the caves as fast as possible.

The island was run through with them, like some kind of giant underground maze. The closest cavern opening they'd found was only a minute's walk up from the beach. But that was during the day, and in the light. Now the cave seemed impossibly far off as they shuffled along, tripping over roots and rocks and squinting through the heaviest downpour Vanessa had ever seen.

"Just keep moving!" she shouted. "It's going to be okay! It's going to be—"

The words caught in her throat with a sob. The truth was, Vanessa had no idea if it was going to be okay or not. How was a thirteen-year-old supposed to handle something like this? Still, Buzz and Carter were eleven, and Jane was only nine. Without any parents or other adults around, it was up to her to keep the three younger ones safe for as long as possible. That much Vanessa knew.

But knowing it and doing it were two very different things.

Carter gritted his teeth. It wasn't as if Vanessa, Buzz, or Jane could see him in the dark, but he knew he had to stay strong. This wasn't a place where you could let your guard down, even for a second.

As they trudged uphill, he kept one hand on his little sister's shoulder and another on the pillowcase he'd used as a makeshift pack. It was heavy with the fire axe from the *Lucky Star*, along with some sea charts and whatever else he'd scooped off the galley table in the dark. There hadn't been time to pick and choose. They'd taken whatever they could before the boat was swept away. Everything else was lost.

Meanwhile, the cold wind off the Pacific seemed to cut right through his soaking-wet clothes. He couldn't stop shivering—and neither could Jane. If there was any good news, it was that the ground had started to level off underfoot. That meant they were getting close.

Sure enough, with the next flash of lightning,

Carter saw just ahead a familiar rock wall and the arched black opening of the cave itself. It was huge, maybe two stories high and wide enough for a truck to turn around inside. It wouldn't be any warmer in there, but at least it would be dry.

"Straight ahead! Did you see that?" he shouted.

No one answered, but they all picked up their pace. The small beam of Vanessa's flashlight led the way across the last twenty yards of flat muddy ground.

As they passed under the rock overhang and into the cave's entrance, Carter felt the rain lighten to a sprinkle, then down to nothing at all. Finally, a break. Vanessa, Jane, and Buzz all sank to the ground, heaving for breath in the dark.

"Keep going!" Carter said. The wind was still bad at the front of the cave. There was no sense stopping now.

"Give us a second," Vanessa told him.

"Just a little farther," Carter said. "It's freezing right here!"

"Um . . . you guys?" Jane said.

"It's freezing everywhere. Calm down!" Vanessa said. Even now, she had to be the boss. It was like she couldn't help it.

"*You* calm down!" Carter snapped, just before Jane cut them both off.

"You guys—*listen!*" she said, louder than before. The urgency in her voice was unmistakable.

"What is it?" Buzz asked.

"There's something in here," Jane said.

Carter ducked his head to listen. The rain outside poured down, but the sounds in the cave seemed to bounce off one another and amplify. And that's when he heard it. A soft rustling of some kind was coming from deeper inside. Something was moving around back there. It sent a fresh wave of goose bumps down his arms.

"Everyone get up . . . slowly," he said. "Vanessa, you got the light?"

"Got it," she said. She'd turned off the flashlight to save the batteries, but she clicked it back on now. The beam shook unsteadily as she played it across the cave walls.

Then, before the light could show them anything, a piercing scream broke out of the darkness. For a split second, Carter thought it was Jane—but she was right there next to him. The sound was farther away than that. And in fact, he realized, it hadn't been a human voice at all. It was an animal.

He and Vanessa looked at each other.

"Run!" Vanessa shouted.

As she turned to go, she tripped and fell. The flashlight dropped out of her hand. In the next moment they were all thrown into inky pitch blackness—just as Carter spotted the shadow of something on four legs bolting straight at them from the back of the cave.

And behind it were several others, all screaming as they came.

Something big slammed into Jane as it ran past her in the dark. It sent a shock wave of pain through her arm. Her hand slipped out of Carter's, and she spun around as she fell, scraping her knees and palms over the rocky ground.

"Carter!" she yelled.

"Jane? Where are you?"

It was impossible to see through the darkness, much less to try to reach her brother. The stampede of beasts—whatever they were—pounded all around them now. Jane could feel their feet thudding on either side of her. She tried to crawl away toward the wall on one side just as one of them raced by. She then moved in the opposite direction, only to be knocked to the ground a second time. There was nowhere to go. All she could do was curl into a ball with her knees drawn up tight, and hope not to get completely trampled.

The worst part was the noise. Even with her hands over her ears, it filled Jane's head—a humanlike, squealing sound straight out of a horror movie. It seemed to go on and on, echoing off the cave walls and high ceiling. She let out a scream of her own, but it only mixed in with the others until she couldn't hear herself at all.

Then, as quickly as it had begun, the sounds faded. The thudding feet grew softer. The squealing came from outside now, and trailed off into the night.

Jane's heart was still pounding when she moved her hands away from her ears and tried to look around.

"Carter?" she said again. "Vanessa? Buzz?"

"I'm here," Carter answered. He was closer than she'd realized. Somehow that made her feel a little better. "Is everyone okay?"

"I'm okay," Buzz said, though his voice sounded shaky.

"Me, too," Vanessa answered. Jane could sense them all crawling toward her, feeling their way, but it was impossible to see.

"Where's the flashlight?" she asked.

A few soft clicking noises came from nearby. And then, "I think it's broken," Vanessa answered.

This wasn't like any darkness Jane had ever experienced at home. Not like when she turned off her bedside light to go to sleep at night. At least then, you could see your hand in front of your face. Here, the only comfort at all came from the sound of the others' voices. As soon as Carter found her, she wrapped her arms around him and held on tight. She squeezed her eyes shut in the dark, trying to cut off the tears, but they wouldn't stop. After everything that had just happened, it was hard not to wonder, *What else? What next?*

Vanessa and Buzz were close behind. They clustered in tightly now with Carter and Jane. All four of them were still shaking badly.

"What were those things, anyway?" Carter asked.

"Wild boars," Jane answered. "That's what they had to be."

She'd seen pictures of them back home, and even a video about boar hunting in the South Pacific. The boars were like wild pigs, big and strong with tusks and sharp teeth. It was lucky none of them had been hurt, or completely trampled. Jane shivered with the thought of what could have happened.

"They were probably trying to get out of the storm, too," she said. "I'll bet we took their spot."

"What if they want it back?" Buzz asked.

"Let's hope they don't," Carter answered. There wasn't much to say to that. All they could really do now was stick close together, wait for daylight, and hope for the best.

As Jane hunkered in with the others, teeth chattering in the dark, wet clothes sticking to her skin, it all started to sink in. These last three days on the island had been the worst of her life, by far. The worst of *any* of their lives. They'd barely had enough food, and they'd practically killed themselves finding water. So far, there had been no sign of rescue, and no way of knowing if help was coming anytime soon. Or at all. It had been just the four of them living alone on the wreck of the *Lucky Star*.

Now even the boat was gone, along with the last of their food and almost everything else they'd had on board. All of which could mean only one thing. Their lives here were about to get harder.

Much, much harder.

LOOK FOR BOOK THREE!

It's been days since Buzz, Vanessa, Carter, and Jane were stranded in the middle of the South Pacific. No adults. No supplies. Nothing but themselves and the jungle. And they've lost their only shelter, and quite possibly their one chance at being rescued. Now they must delve even deeper into Nowhere Island for food and supplies. But the island has a few secrets of its own to tell. . . . With danger at every turn, this blended family has to learn how to trust one another if they stand any chance of survival.

GET LOST IN MORE ADVENTURE WITH

Book 1: **FORBIDDEN PASSAGE**

Book 2: **THE SABOTAGE**

Book 3: **DESPERATE MEASURES**